THE TRUE MEN

MARY Q. STEELE

The True Men

GREENWILLOW BOOKS
A DIVISION OF WILLIAM MORROW & COMPANY, INC.
NEW YORK

1 2 3 4 5   80 79 78 77 76

Library of Congress Cataloging
in Publication Data
Steele, Mary Q
The True Men.
Summary: Expelled by his people because he has been stricken with an
unusual "affliction" which sets him apart
from others, a youth begins a search for
a place of his own in the world.
[1. Prejudices—Fiction] I. Title.
PZ7.S8146Tr [Fic] 76-5482
ISBN 0-688-80052-1
ISBN 0-688-84052-3 lib. bdg.

THE TRUE MEN

1

As soon as the sun slid within a hand's breadth of the horizon Ree knew it without looking up from his work. He had always been good at judging the passing of time. Even on a starless cloudy night, waking he would know at once that it was midnight or an hour before dawn or minutes before the time he must rise and begin the day.

It was fortunate that he had this ability. It had always been a convenience and now it was a necessity. Without it he would have been found out long ago, days ago, probably when he himself had first begun to notice what was happening. He shivered.

For sooner or later he would be discovered, he knew that. Now he could hide. It was sometimes difficult, but he could manage. Nevertheless the True Men would not stay here many days more. When the ceremonies were over, when the council had finished their consultations, they would move on once again, and he would be found out. For often as not they traveled after dark. Sometimes all night the little ponies plodded, the small bells jingled, the high-wheeled carts rolled.

There would be no way to hide then.

He would not think of it. When it happened it happened, and until it happened he would try not to fret about it. What was there to do? Nothing. Not one thing.

Yet he was frightened, terribly frightened.

Now he gathered the last of the lather leaves from the plant he had come across and thrust them inside his shirt. His family would be pleased. There were enough to last a long time and they were big, they would make suds in plenty.

His pony was already loaded with peats for the fire and roots for baking and boiling and a great wad of vibon hair. He had been lucky to find so much in one day.

He glanced at the sky and then tugged on the pony's lead. His route back to the camp took him close to the Council Ring, the circle of red sand inside which people might stand or sit to hear what the council had to say, to ask questions and petition help for problems.

This circle, of course, was different. Larger, and more carefully cleared of stones and underbrush, and in its very center stood the House of Houses; Ree had seen it only once in his life before, a canopy of fine soft skins and woven cloths in bright designs. Inside, hidden by the tapestries and pelts, the council consulted together and in their midst lay all those things which Ree's people valued above others as the lark's song soars above the cricket's: the bone plate with its mysterious symbols that marked the pact between earth and the True Men and gave them the High Plains for their own; and the nine silvery pieces of stone, shaped roughly like men, which had fallen from the sky when the comet first appeared, in the beginning of time, and had caused the council to be created. These things made the True Men themselves, different from other people, happier, more fortunate.

Three or four times a year the council met, but now they had made the larger ring and set up the House of Houses because the comet had once again appeared in the sky. Their comet. Once again the sign of affirmation. There would be celebrations and feasting. Ree did not stop to look at any of this or wonder what the council was planning. He'd have to hurry, for clouds were gathering along the edge of the sky. If they moved across the sun . . .

The clouds stayed where they were, there was a gold-rose light of sunset over the world while he unloaded the pony and hobbled it for the night. Poor pony. The grazing here was surely not of the best. Still, someone had put out hay in bundles. The ponies would manage.

Ree piled the peats and the roots in the communal heaps at the side of the camp, but the vibon hair and the lather leaves he took with him to his mother's dwelling. She was stooping over the fire as he came up, and when she straightened he stared at her for a second, seeing her as though he had been absent for years instead of a single day.

How small she was! Surely only lately had she grown so stooped, almost hunchbacked. And those lines on her forehead, like scars. He did not remember ever seeing them before and yet, thinking back, he could not remember a time when she did not have them.

When he was found out, would she grow more bent? Would those marks across her face deepen and lengthen? Thinking of it, he wanted to cry to her, "I couldn't help it, Mali. It isn't my fault. I couldn't help it."

But he said no word. Instead he handed her the lather leaves, and she held them up exclaiming, "Oh, what great big ones! I haven't seen any like these in many a day. And vibon hair! How long and fine it is. Thank you, Ree."

"Is supper ready?" he asked. "Can I have mine now?"

"Yes, of course," she answered. "But won't you wait? The others will be here soon. Even your father will be back from the council in a bit. You haven't seen him for three days. And Merma will be angry. She said you promised her a present."

Ree smiled. The thought of his younger sister Merma always made him smile. But he took a bowl and spooned some stew into it and sat down to eat.

"I'm tired," he answered. "I've traveled a long way today. I'll sleep now and see my father in the morning. And give Merma her present."

Mali stepped toward him and put her hand on his head as he sat by the fire. She turned his face up to hers and looked into his eyes.

"Are you not well?" she asked. "For a week now you've been wrapped in your blanket before sundown. And . . ."

She broke off, but Ree knew what she meant. He had tried to behave naturally, as though nothing were wrong. He was not good at deceiving. And it would seen strange to almost anyone, the way he took his blanket and went away from the camp before dusk.

What else could he do? What else could he do? Now he pulled his head away from under his mother's hand.

"I'm all right," he answered almost sulkily, and finished his stew. He mopped out the bowl with hearth bread. Mali said nothing more.

Ree was hungry and would have liked more stew,

but the sun was setting fast, he dared not wait. As long as he was in the glow of the fire, as long as the gleam of day hung in the sky, he was safe. It was darkness he feared, and darkness was coming quickly. He sprang up, seized his blanket and slung it across his shoulders.

"I'm for bed," he said, smiling at his mother, trying to be only Ree, son of Mali and Ginda, not the person to whom this terrible thing had happened. "Tell my father I look forward to seeing him tomorrow. And Merma and my brother."

Mali smiled back, though her eyes were full of worry. He knew she would watch him as he walked away. Carelessly he let the blanket slide down his back, almost covering him, and then he went quickly into the gathering twilight.

He found a spot behind a rock, where he had slept for two nights previously. The branches of small evergreens that he had broken off and piled there were still fresh and spicy-smelling. He wrapped his blanket securely around him and lay down.

And only just in time. The sun was a tiny tiny red crescent on the world's rim. Darkness came rolling over the sandy earth and the stands of scrubby bushes and the wind-carved rocks. Ree pulled his blanket over his head.

He hoped he was safe. Sometimes other people roamed around, seeking a place to sleep away from the fires and the stamping ponies and the sounds of households.

Through the small opening he had made for his nose and eyes, he lay watching the shadows deepen. He could see one star in the deep blue-green sky. It would be clear tomorrow, cloudless and clear. A night bird called, a soft sweet purring note, a chuckling note, as though it found the coming of darkness a delight, could scarcely wait for the night and the beginning of its time of living.

Ree sighed. It was not that way for him. He hated the dark. It was true he was tired, for he rose early and walked far and fast, hoping to fall asleep as soon as he lay down, hoping to put everything out of his mind. But he was seldom able to do it. He was too worried. He could not believe it was happening and that it was getting worse. Every day it got worse.

He groaned softly to himself. What could it mean? What should he do? Those were the things he asked himself a million times a day, and there was never an answer. Never an answer.

Sometimes he considered telling Mali and Ginda. Perhaps they would know what to do. Perhaps the council would know what to do. The council knew much. Perhaps it was not as terrible as he imagined it to be. Perhaps it was something which had happened before, a simple matter easily put right. Perhaps his fears had been for nothing . . .

He groaned again. Deceiving himself was simple enough, but in his heart he recognized the deception. There was no help for him. There would be no help for him. Fear and sorrow made him tremble under his blanket.

He turned his eyes a little and there was the glow in the sky, near the horizon. The comet. The True Men's comet. The sign in the heavens that they were indeed the True Men and possessed of wisdom beyond other peoples'.

The sight of the comet calmed him after a while. What happened to Ree, son of Mali and Ginda, was only a little thing compared to the fate of a whole race, a good people living a good life. He thought of that life, of the gentle warm summers spent on the High Plains, the land that belonged to the True Men, that had been given them in a pact with the earth itself. They worked hard there and raised crops and made their stores of food. The air was clear and bright, the birds sang, the sun was warm—and it was theirs. Even when the icy wind began to blow and the True Men gathered themselves and their belongings and their winter supplies into their little carts and descended into the valleys where they had no home— even then they led a brave happy life, remembering the High Plains and that they would return there. And now in the sky the comet had appeared once more this winter. Only a faint glow, but those who remembered said that soon it would sweep like fire across the sky, trailing its glory behind it like a bright and golden scarf.

It was a time for rejoicing and happiness and strength. Only Ree walked in fear by day and huddled in fear by night. Only Ree carried in his heart an icy needle of pain. Staring at the comet, he thought of these things over and over, until after a long while he fell asleep.

Nevertheless he woke early, before dawn, and was restless, longed to get out of his blanket and be away, be busy, be doing things, anything. He dared not stir, not till the land was full of light. At last he flung aside his blanket and rose and walked toward his family's hearthfire.

Others were up and beginning the daily tasks as he walked by, one or two of them glanced at him curiously. Or at any rate they seemed to glance curiously. Most only spoke a word or raised a hand in greeting, and none of them stopped him or questioned him. It was all right, he told himself. Another day and it was all right.

Today he would go looking for more vibon hair. Yesterday he had seen tracks as though a great herd had crossed through the little copse where he had come upon the lather leaves. Now, near the end of the winter weather, the beasts would be shedding their heavy pelts. There would be plenty of hair for him to gather and bring home for spinning. Mali and Ginda would be pleased.

He raised his head and glanced across the whole camp at his own fireside where his parents would be waiting. He halted and stared in consternation and then in terror.

He would run. He could still run. He knew a place, not too far, a small cave into which he had ventured once or twice. He could run and before anyone could follow he could be out of sight and then hidden away in the cave. They would not find him. No one else knew of it, the entrance was cunningly concealed.

What good would it do for him to run? He couldn't run away from what had happened. Nothing would change that. If he had gone at once, when it first began, before anyone else knew, he might have spared his family something. Something, he was not sure what.

Now it was too late. Now he had waited too long. For there beside Mali's cooking fire, gathered round with grave faces, stood his mother and his father and Kadir, the head of the council, and two other council members. And Kadir was wearing, over his head and shoulders, the Black Mantle of Grief!

2

REE STOOD quite still. His mother had seen him and was watching, her eyes were wide and solemn in a white terror-stricken face. After a minute she touched Ginda's arm and he turned and gazed too at his older son, Ree, whose name meant arrow because he was swift in going where he was directed to go.

Finally Ginda moved toward him. He stood a dozen feet away and asked softly, "Ree? Are you all right?"

"Of course I'm all right," Ree answered. He had not meant to speak in such a harsh, almost defiant tone. "Why shouldn't I be all right?" He paused and then spoke again, sounding frightened. "What do you mean, am I all right?"

No one answered. Kadir, in his strange black cloak,

and the other two council members came to stand just behind Ginda. Ree folded his blanket closely about him, though the sun was warm enough. Everyone was turning now, everyone in the camp had noticed Kadir's mantle and that something strange, something extraordinary, was taking place. Three other members of the council came swiftly up to the hearth.

"Ree, the council wishes to speak with you. Will you come now to the Council Ring and talk with the whole council?"

There was no point in answering. Ree would not have refused, even if he had known how. The council was never refused anything, and what could Ree, a boy not grown to full height or to a man's knowledge, say to all these grave adults? Kadir walked up and laid a hand on his arm, and Ree went, with Mali and Ginda and the other council members following.

The meeting place was not far. Ree could see the canopied House of Houses silhouetted against the pale sky. Kadir's hand on his arm was gentle but firm, and they went quickly and steadily on until they were inside the ring and then standing before the House.

"Come inside," Kadir urged.

Ree hung back. "Can we not speak out here, in the open air?" he asked. Kadir looked around irritably and Ree thought he had made the council head angry.

But Kadir asked, "Where are Emla and Datri? They should be here. The whole council should be here."

Ginda answered, "They went early this morning to

fetch water from the healing springs, for Emla's son. His fever had got worse." He looked distraught. Ree's heart thumped slowly in his chest and he turned his head and stared across the plain and up toward the mountains.

"Yes, I forgot," muttered Kadir. "I should not have let them go. But then yesterday I did not know." His face under the Black Mantle was lined and worried. "Perhaps we should wait for them. And then perhaps not."

Mali cried out suddenly, "Kadir, I cannot wait. Tell me now! Why have you come for my son? What is wrong? Have we done something wrong that you fetch him away while you hide under the Black Mantle? What is it?"

"You must forgive me, Mali," said Kadir. "I am the head of the council. I am responsible for whatever good or bad befalls the True Men. I cannot hide what I know about Ree and Ree cannot hide it. The whole council should be here and all the people should know, so that we can move wisely. But something must be done, I think, and done quickly."

He lifted the draperies and once more took Ree by the arm and pushed the boy before him.

"Come," he bade the others and they came inside, Kadir and Ginda and Mali and the five other council members.

When they were all inside, Kadir let the hangings fall and they stood in darkness. And yet not in darkness. For there was a light in the little canopy, a soft luster sufficient to show the faces of the councilmen and women. Ree covered his eyes with his hands. He could not bear to see the way Mali and the others stared at him.

"Wh-what is it?" Ginda stammered. No one answered. Ree took his hands from his face and gazed down at them, at the strange light that shimmered away from him as though he had fire instead of blood in his veins. In the dimness under the tent his whole body glistened like foxfire.

What a horrible thing, to be diseased this way! It had begun so gradually. Waking in the night, he had noticed how his hands and arms looked in the dark. Something there and not quite there. So that looking directly he could not see it, only out of the corner of his eye was he sure about the strange sheen. Even then he pretended it wasn't so. It was reflection from one of the campfires, still glowing. It was the result of rubbing his arms with the resin of a kula tree, to heal cuts and scratches. It was . . .

It was something terribly, horribly wrong. Every night it got worse, his skin gleamed brighter and brighter. He began to sleep far away from his own fireside, going to bed at sundown with his blanket pulled over his head, for he thought his face must be affected too, although he couldn't see it.

He was safe in the day, but at night, as soon as the sun was gone from the sky, the luminescence began, the eerie coppery light that came from nowhere but his own red-brown skin . . .

Sooner or later someone would discover his secret, would find him out. He had known all along. He had dreaded that moment, and yet at the same time he had longed for it. He didn't want to be the only one to know this monstrous secret. He wanted to shout it. He wanted to tell anyone, anyone at all, but he didn't know whom or how to tell.

And now it was known. Now it was a secret no longer. He trembled and wished it were a secret still.

"How did you find this out?" Ginda asked Kadir abruptly.

"Last night I could not sleep," the head of the council answered. "I walked about and came on Ree asleep in his blanket. And as I passed, he turned and flung out a hand. I saw it and pulled the blanket a little way from his head and shoulders. I did not wake him. There was no need. And there was so much to think about . . ."

There was a long silence. When Kadir spoke again, his voice was grieving and haunted. "When I was chosen head of the council, I was hopeful. It is an honor—still it is a burden too, and I hoped that I might be brave and strong, and when my time was done I hoped the True Men might be as they have ever been, a people to whom earth and sky themselves have spoken and given much to be proud of. It was all I hoped. I had not thought about the comet."

Ree supposed that was likely so. Though on many nights during his life he himself, like others of the True Men, had swept his eyes across the sky for a glimpse of the comet, he had not really thought to see it. The comet came at long intervals, and when it wanted. No one could know when or expect or hope for it.

"But it came!" cried Kadir passionately. "The comet came, while I was head of the council!"

Ree remembered the night, the glad songs that had risen up to the far-off sky visitor. He remembered how the oldest ones had gathered to tell tales, for though they had not seen it before themselves, their parents had. They knew it would appear there in the sky, faint and close to the earth's edge, and that it would grow and grow until, when it was over the High Plains, it would be a spectacle such as none of them had beheld before, a glory of the sky. It had been a joyful occasion.

Nevertheless there had been unease too, a little edge of anxiety and uncertainty. The comet had not in their memory appeared in the winter. The cold months had been hard and there was little food left for the feasting and celebrations with which the True Men were pledged to greet the comet. There had been a strange ague and fever among them, some had died, many had been ill and were long recovering. A cold thin sad time.

No wonder Kadir had been worried and sleepless. His name would be remembered as head of the council in the year the comet returned to the True Men and could not be properly welcomed.

Ree was sorry for Kadir. But what had it all to do with him? And the thing that had happened to him? Was it a new kind of fever? Did Kadir propose to send for healing waters for Ree? Was there any help for him?

As if in answer to Ree's thoughts, Kadir said bitterly, "And now this." He gestured toward Ree. "This curse or disease or whatever it is . . . " He broke off and looked angrily around as if for someone to rescue him from having to solve an insoluble riddle.

And Mali cried, "Curse? Why is it a curse? Or a disease?"

"What else would you name it?" Kadir almost shouted. "Have you ever seen such a thing before? Or heard of it? Is this—this change in him like any change in man or beast or stone that you know of? I have no knowledge of it. I do not know what to do about it."

He gestured toward Ree. "I only know this boy must leave. If he were my own child, I would send him away. He is no longer one of the True Men. Whatever has happened to him has happened to him alone. He is a stranger to us. Now we must be one people and act as one people and think as one people. If we could help him, we would help him. But if we cannot help him, then he must do what he can to help us. He must go away."

Ree was terrified. In his heart he had not supposed

the council and Kadir could do anything for him. Whatever his affliction was, he had been sure he must bear it alone. But he had supposed they would give him support and friendship and whatever wisdom they could summon up. And now to be despised and driven away! He could scarcely believe it. The True Men did not do such things. They had gone mad.

In his fear he spoke out angrily to Kadir, as he would not otherwise have dared to do.

"You think I am a demon!" he cried. "Or else you think I can bear away the fever and the bad weather on my back, the way some people load a donkey or a goat with sticks and drive it out into the wilderness to carry trouble with it. You have forgot I am Ree, one of the True Men, born on the High Plains!"

Kadir's face knotted with feeling. Ree could not see what the man was really thinking. For a moment he thought the council head was going to strike him.

"The True Men are not foolish and ignorant," Kadir said at last with dignity. "They know that each one of us must bear his own burden of wickedness and stupidity, as he must learn to share the burden of all. They know they cannot get rid of their ills by piling them on a poor goat's back.

"Our troubles have nothing to do with you. They are our own troubles, grown worse for a while as chance sometimes decrees. Now the fever is lessening. Soon the season will turn, it will be spring. These things will come about, for that is the way the world is ordered.

"But this—this is not the way the world is ordered." Kadir's voice was hoarse, as though the words were almost too hurtful to say. "The one to whom this has happened has been marked out. No longer one of the True Men. I do not know why. Now when we must not be divided, but must be one whole, I dare not let you stay. I must send you away."

There was a sort of sense to it. Despairingly Ree looked around at the others. There was a sort of sense to it—he saw it in the faces of all of them, even in the faces of Mali and Ginda. They sorrowed for him, they hated and feared to see him go—and yet, they knew he must. Kadir was speaking as wisely as he could, and Kadir was a man of no little wisdom.

Ree said nothing more. Kadir laid a hand on his shoulder and went on more kindly, "We will wait for Emla and Datri. The whole council will decide. We will decide what is best for you to do and help you in what small way we can."

They went away. Ree sat alone in the House of Houses. He huddled under his blanket and waited for the minutes to pass and watched the pale glimmer of his own two hands.

Ree carried his blanket, his knife with the metal blade, and a small packet of food. Mali had given him the food—some boiled roots, a little bread, and even a few dried fruits and some nuts. It would mean that Mali and Ginda would have almost nothing to contribute to the feast when the comet swung over the High Plains, a feast that would be spare enough at best.

Did it mean also they loved him still, in spite of what had happened to him, in spite of the council's decision? He raised his eyes to Mali's and saw there sorrow and bewilderment and fear, as she must see in his. If there was something more, he could not tell what it was.

She stepped forward and put her arms for a moment around him.

"Good-bye," she whispered. "Perhaps you will find another home. Perhaps you will—" she broke off and stepped away.

Ginda too hugged him slightly and Fadan, his dreamy young brother, who did not seem to know what was happening. Ree leaned down and kissed Merma, his sister.

Funny Merma, who could always make him laugh, telling him long stories about stones and blades of grass that gossiped with each other and made plans for weddings or argued over the proper way to cook apples. Merma, who could do a dance of the vibon, raising her narrow shoulders, letting her head and long hair droop forward, swaying back and forth, heavy-footed and solemn, turning a thin little girl into a great hairy slow beast. Good-bye to Merma.

Kadir took his hand. "I am sorry," the council head said. His voice was truly heavy with sorrow. Was it for Ree or for the True Men or for Kadir? "I wish you well. It is a thing that happened. I am sorry that it happened to you."

That was true. It had been a chance thing. And chance ruled the True Men, as Ree knew. The members of the council were chosen by lot, and when in their travels the caravan moved from place to place and came to a crossroads, Kadir threw the journey stick and they went as it pointed.

Kadir would not throw the journey stick now. Ree was no longer considered one of the True Men. He might go where he liked as long as he did not travel to the High Plains. All directions were his as long as he went—and went quickly.

"Good-bye," he said and gazed once more at Ginda and Mali. And then he set out. He did not turn around, but suddenly a sound of running made him stop. A hand grasped his and he looked down at Merma.

"Ree," she said softly. "When you come home, bring me a present from a faraway place."

He watched her small face.

Forget me, little sister, he wanted to say. Forget me and the pebbles and shells I have brought you before. I will not come here again. Forget me altogether.

Instead he put his hand on her cheek for a second before he walked on.

"Remember me," he murmured.

3

REE STARED out across the wide valley. Compared to the High Plains, it was dull country, dimly colored, shadowed, indefinite. The land fell gently into long low basins, filled with marshes and small lakes, and then rose up little knobby hills, covered with scrubby undergrowth, and dropped slowly back again.

And yet Ree loved it. Here every winter of his life he had wandered with the True Men and he was familiar with much of it, in spite of its great size.

He knew that the dark smudge there a few miles away marked a herd of vibon, and though he could not see them, he knew that tiny brown hawks hovered above them, crying Kitter! Kitter! in low voices as they waited for insects stirred up by the hoofs of the beasts.

He knew that the dust in the other direction was caused by the goats and sheep of one of the tribes of wanderers who drove their flocks hither and thither all year in the valley, looking for forage. Poor scrawny animals, poor sad people, always moving from place to place, scarcely bothering even to shelter themselves from the weather.

I am like that now, Ree thought.

For three days he had been stumbling aimlessly across the countryside. He had gone in a daze, not heeding where he was going. Surely someone would come after him. Surely the True Men, who lived in kindness and goodness, surely they would not turn away from him.

But no one came. And after three days the numbness began to drain away and anger took its place.

Now he was coming into a different sort of region, a place he had never been before or seen its like. It was rocky and bare, and all a strange grim yellow color. The valley held many colors, olive and dusty green, gray-blue and lavender, rusty brown and tan. Not bright colors but mild and, Ree thought, beautiful.

Here the color offended him and the bare rocks looked awkward and uneasy, as though they might suddenly start rolling toward him. It was the edge of the valley and beyond it lay another part of the world. The True Men, some of them, went out into that world now and again, only on rare errands and always glad to return. Now Ree was going, bent only on leaving the valley and the High Plains and the True Men behind forever. His people were mad, demented, all of them. He would put them out of his mind.

A trail of sorts led upward among the rocks. It was not a well-worn path, the place where it led must be an obscure place. Those who walked this way were few in number and did not often make the journey. It seemed to Ree that such a road and such a destination must suit him.

He began to climb.

He heard the people ahead of him long before he saw them. The sounds of their voices and the clopping of their animals' feet echoed and grew among the rocks and came to him so clearly that he thought surely he would see them around this bend or this one or the next. But night came and he had not sighted them and did not want to.

He went a long way from the trail and lay down on a smooth boulder and pulled his blanket close about him. Everything he did now, he did by daylight. No one would ever learn Ree's secret, not ever again. By night he would hide if he had to dig a grave for himself to hide in.

In the dark he heard the loud laugh of a hanhan dog high away above him, but he was not afraid. Everyone knew hanhan dogs were cowards. This one would not come near. He lay there thinking of Mali and Ginda, and trying not to. He did not want to think about those who had sent him away from them, let him go without stretching a hand to hold him back.

I would not go back anyway, he said to himself bitterly. Nothing can make me go back. I will not think of them.

The late winter sun was well above the rim of the valley when he woke. It meant he did not have as early a start as he would have liked. Those who make a journey should take advantage of good weather and begin the day when the day begins. He was surprised therefore when after very little walking he came upon the people he had followed yesterday, still sleeping around a dead campfire. He stood watching them, until he noticed that one or two of them were watching him.

"Good day," he said politely and began to walk past. One of the watchers, a boy not much older than Ree, sprang up from his pallet and came toward him.

He was taller than Ree but very thin and wiry. He was not like anyone Ree had ever seen before, not like the wandering herdsmen of the valley, or like the men who sometimes came hunting vibon, or like the True Men. His skin and eyes and hair were all the same color, sand-colored. He was sleek and pale.

"Good day," said the stranger. "Sit down and we will eat."

"I have eaten," answered Ree, for he had indeed, some of the hard bread and boiled roots Mali had given him. Up till last night he had found his own food in the valley. Not very good and not very much, but sufficient. Last night he had been grateful for his thrift. He had not had to search for supper in that barren place, or make a fire to cook it.

Then he added, "But I am thirsty. Have you something to drink?" The other boy gestured. "There's a spring, I'll show you."

Together they wandered off among the crags. The rest of the camp was beginning to stir and the fire smoldered as a woman fed it dry stalks of grass.

The spring was not far and the water was good. Ree wished he might take some with him.

He followed the strange boy, back to the fire leaping now under a pot suspended from a metal tripod. There were ten or so adults and four or five children of various ages, and a baby who wept sadly and softly. They had beasts of burden, two big grouchy-looking humpbacked dondaris and a horse. There was a small roofed cart, like the ones the True Men used, not so well made and sturdy. And to one side another wheeled box, with bars along the side. Ree could not imagine what it was for. Most of the group paid no attention to him, but one of the men called out, "Are you one of those who call themselves the True Men?"

"No," Ree answered, and it was not a lie. He was one of them no longer.

But the word was hard to say. His tongue still found it a lie.

The man laughed. "Good. For they must be fools, to speak of themselves so. True Men! We are all true men, I say, if we walk the earth for a while and eat and sleep and then die."

For a moment Ree was angry. He wanted to speak out and tell how the earth itself had made a pact with the True Men and given them the High Plains and set the comet in the sky to remind them that of all the world's peoples only the True Men had been so honored. Instead he bit his lip and stared at the fire.

"Where are you going?" the man asked, and Ree thought quickly.

"To the Stone Towns," he responded, for it was the answer that came into his head. Besides, whoever climbed these mountains must sooner or later almost certainly come to one of the Stone Towns. They rimmed the wide valley on this side. Several of the strangers stared at him curiously.

"Then you've taken a queer way to go," said the man.

"Where are you going?" countered Ree hastily.

"Ha! Back where we came from," answered the man in anger and disgust.

Ree did not inquire where that might be. The fewer questions he asked, the fewer he need feel obligated to answer. Still he wondered mightily why the man thought this way to the Stone Towns queerer than any other.

"I must go," he said finally and turned to the trail.

"I'll walk with you," said the strange boy. There was

certainly no way for Ree to refuse. They climbed together up among the yellow rocks.

"Do you really mean to go to the Stone Towns?" asked the boy.

Ree nodded.

"Then why did you not take some other path?" the stranger wanted to know. Ree pondered a little. It might not be the wisest thing to say he had not known there was any other path. Something about this boy, about all these people, made him uneasy.

"I wanted to take this path," he said stubbornly. "It was closer."

The boy stared. "You must be too brave for your own good," he said at last. "They say the earth still shakes there in the pass, and the ground has holes that open up, and most of the houses are gone. Most of the people too, and only the ghosts of those who died when the houses collapsed run up and down the streets."

Ree was too startled not to speak. "The Stone Towns are gone?" he asked breathlessly.

The other boy was impatient, "No, only those in this pass, where the world shivered till the stones rolled down the mountainsides. It hasn't been so long ago, everyone knows about it. The other towns are still there, but if you take this path, you must go through the pass to get to them."

Ree walked on, staring down at the trail as he walked. He said at last, slowly and carefully, "Then you too must be brave; all of you and the carts and the dondaris, won't you have to cross the pass as I will have to?"

"Not us," the other boy answered. "We are not going to the Stone Towns at all. We take another trail, and always have, even before the ground shook. Now we couldn't get the carts over the fallen rocks, we've heard. And my father doesn't want to give the toll they ask from people who use the pass." He grinned.

The people of the Stone Towns had never foraged or hunted or farmed. From those who traveled through the passes they exacted a toll, so much grain or food or vibon hair. It was the people of the Stone Towns who did the hard work of keeping the roads clear and smooth and easily traveled.

And too, they acted as carriers and messengers and vendors. They were sturdy people who did not mind driving goats up the steep paths or bearing loads of vibon meat from one side of the mountain across the ridges and down the other. Many people in both valleys found it easier to stay at home with their flocks or their farms and let the people of the Stone Towns do their fetching and carrying. And for the service the men of the Stone Towns received a portion of the goods.

It had always been so. Ree was glad he had not been born in the Stone Towns. A hard way to live, among the hard stones.

And then the boy added thoughtfully, "Still my

father might decide to go by himself to the pass and see what can be seen. If there are truly ghosts, it may be he can find some use for them. They say, too, that melted rocks poured down the slopes out of a hole in the ground. My father might make use of that too. He's clever. And especially now he might go, since we've come a long way and have to go back empty-handed."

Ree wished he had the courage to confess that he did not know what use this boy's father would make of ghosts or molten stone, that he wanted very much to know what these people had come into the wide valley seeking and had to leave without obtaining. He wanted to know just because he wanted to know, for he realized already that he did not wish to have any part of their plans or their travels or their kind of life. He would be glad when the path divided and they could go their separate ways.

And yet, curiosity about them scraped away at him so that he almost asked. Only the fear that the other boy would press him, Ree, about where he was going and where he had come from stopped him.

The stranger slid his oddly colored eyes sidewise and watched Ree, smiling a little to himself. And then he burst into a jeering laugh.

"You don't think my father would want such things, do you? You don't know what he would do with them? Ah, my father's clever, and my mother too. We travel about, you see, and come into towns and my mother has potions and amulets for those who want them and my father has cures of every kind. He can make cures for rheumatism from the melted rock and cures for anything from a ghost, if he could catch one." He walked on a minute and then added glumly, "That's why we're here. One of those wanderers in the valley came to tell us he had a goat born with two heads. We came with the cage to take it away, but it died and was eaten before we got there. My father likes to have such things about. People come to see. And creatures like that reek of magic. And even if it had died, my mother could have made many charms from the hair and flesh of a two-headed goat."

Ree was horrified. The True Men would never have made use of such silly things. There was no magic except the magic of good water and green growing things and the wheel of the day and the seasons. Chance chose whom to strike down with illness or with an accident. There were the waters of some springs which would help in curing and the leaves and flowers of some herbs. But chance would choose who would heal and who would not. Potions and amulets were nonsense.

He turned his head away and stared off among the boulders. No wonder he had distrusted these people as soon as he saw them. He had heard about them many times. They did not believe, either, in their magic drinks and talismans. They merely pretended to, so that they could persuade some bent old man to give them a blanket of vibon hair or a sack of dried fruits for a bit of red stone or a twist of hair supposed to cure his aching joints. Many were foolish enough to be taken in by their conjury. But many besides the True Men despised them.

Only after Ree and the stranger had walked a long while in silence did the thought come to him that he was in great danger. If these people traveled with him till nightfall, they might discover his secret. And if they valued a two-headed goat, how much more would they value a human boy whose skin in the dark glowed like the ashes of a campfire!

4

HE WALKED ON. He might
hurry ahead of this strange boy, but likely the boy
would hurry with him. And how would he explain his
hurry? Why would he wish to get to the Stone Towns
in such a rush?

The stranger was already suspicious of Ree, who had
denied being one of the True Men though it was obviously a lie. Anything Ree did would make him more
inquisitive. If Ree slowed his pace, no doubt the other
boy would do so too. Besides, the whole lot of them
climbed the path below, waiting for him if he should
fall back.

Ree thought about the wheeled box. It must have
been meant to hold the two-headed goat. Would these
people put Ree inside, to exhibit him like a monster,

if they discovered his secret? And if, from behind the bars, he cried for help, would anyone listen? Would anyone try to help him escape? He thought not. Not people who had come to see wonders and magic.

He glanced at the sun. He had a few hours left. Perhaps the path would soon divide and these "conjurers" leave him. Or perhaps they would stop to let the dondaris graze, if any pasturage appeared on the slopes. He hadn't much hope of that. The rocks were as yellow and bare as ever.

Something would surely happen. Something must happen.

The boy spoke abruptly, "You must come from some very far-off place, not to have heard the earthquakes that shook down the rocks into the pass."

"I heard them," answered Ree. "And felt them too, a little. But I was across the valley. And earthquakes happen in the mountains, one doesn't pay too much heed."

"These were different," the stranger said. "Very fierce, and the ground opened and molten rock bubbled out. Some people say it was the coming of the comet which caused it," he added thoughtfully.

Once more Ree was angry. The comet did not come to harm. It came only to remind the True Men that the High Plains were theirs forever and ever, as long as they remained the True Men and remembered their pact with the earth.

After a minute he forced himself to say quietly, "I

should think the comet was too far away to cause such things. And there are often earthquakes."

He glanced again at the sun and then along the bare ugly slopes, looking for a sign that the path branched, or for some object he could pursue or travel toward that would take him off the trail and away from these people. But he saw nothing.

From farther down the slope he heard the squeaky honk of a dondari. The caravan was not so far behind as he had hoped. He quickened his step a little bit. If he should decide simply to run, it would be easier escaping from this single sand-colored boy than from those men, who might even use the dondaris to chase him.

"I'm thirsty again," he said suddenly. "Do you know another spring?"

"There's no water," the boy answered. "Not this side of the mountain rim. My mother will have filled a firkin at the spring. If you wait, they'll catch up with us and you can drink perhaps, if she has brought enough."

If you wait, they'll catch up with us, Ree repeated the words to himself. What the boy meant was, If you wait, I'll wait with you. What he meant was, We are not going to be easy to get away from.

Ree climbed on. The path was very steep here. He could not walk as fast as he would have liked and the sun seemed to race across the sky.

If only he had not chosen this path. If only he had

not . . . There was no use thinking such things. He was alone and in danger and he had been for a long time. He would not be more frightened now than he had been those nights sleeping behind the rock near his family's camp. What happened, happened.

Suddenly a hanhan dog began to yelp and cackle far up the mountain, and another answered and then another. Ree was surprised. Hanhan dogs commonly slept during the day. Only at night they called back and forth in their mad laughing voice—hanhanhanhan-hanhahahaaa. Why were they calling now, more and more of them?

The strange boy stopped and listened too. They waited there on the path and a sound like faraway thunder began to fill in the space between the sharp barks of the hanhan dogs, began to grow and tilt toward them from the mountaintop.

The sand-colored boy turned paler than ever.

"An earthquake!" he shouted. "There's going to be an earthquake!"

The ground slipped softly under Ree's feet, a curious smoky odor filled the air.

The boy spun around and ran down the way they had come. Ree almost followed. He did not want to be alone in an earthquake. He had heard terrible tales before now of what happened when the world shook.

But then he turned and ran the other way. Desperately, staggering among the boulders, expecting any second to have them drop on top of him, feeling the ground quiver more and more, he scrambled up the mountain. Higher and higher until he could no longer keep on, until his breath came in great moaning gasps between his dry lips.

He dropped in the trail where he stood and lay with his face against the bare track and heard the earth moan too, deep inside itself as it bent and struggled and shivered. Under his hands it slid and shook, and he shouted in his fear—it was going to dissolve under his fingers and he was going to fall away into space, into endless air and fall, fall, fall . . .

Something crashed above him. He heard it come bounding and clattering toward him. It would crush him surely, one of the great rocks shaken loose and leaping down the mountain toward him.

But the sounds stopped somewhere higher up, and then at last a few pebbles rolled down the slope and settled against his shoulder, and by and by everything was still.

Ree lay without moving, his heart pounded and pounded, and he was afraid to move. He had not known it would be so terrible, the awful feeling of the world losing its firmness and solidness and crumbling into nothingness beneath his body. He was afraid that if he stood up it would happen once more.

He remembered the men and the dondaris in the caravan, and he wanted to move, but he could not bring himself to turn his head for fear he would disturb the world's balance and set it rocking and shuddering again.

Anyway he supposed the conjurers were as frightened as he was. Or perhaps more so. The sand-colored boy had seemed almost witless. Perhaps they and their animals and their carts would stop a long time where they were before continuing on their way. He did not think they would trouble themselves with Ree. Or at least he hoped so.

After a while he got to his hands and knees slowly, carefully. Nothing happened. He spoke to himself scornfully, telling himself that he could no more cause the earth to quake than the comet could. He must get up and hurry on and hide. Before dark he must be well away from those people in the caravan or from anyone else.

Yet he could not bring himself to stand. On his hands and knees still, he crawled upward and upward. By every huge rock he paused, thinking he might creep behind it and hide. But each one loomed over him, threatening to totter and roll down on him. When he had crept a long way, he stopped and forced himself to pull his body upright. He put his hand on one of the rocks and felt its hardness and the sharp edges of it. It was reassuring somehow, and he stood there while his heart ceased to race in his chest and he felt less afraid.

He walked on, every now and then pausing to listen

for the sounds of anyone coming behind him. He heard nothing at all except a little wind high up along the cliffs. No bird or insect called, the hanhan dogs had hushed, the earth was silent.

Ree climbed the path. In a little time, before it got dark, he would leave the track and take shelter, carefully.

And then suddenly he came to the fork in the road. He was pleased and relieved, until he remembered that he did not know which trail led to the ruined pass and which to the conjurers' secret way through the mountains.

Here was no time to throw a journey stick. Here was a time when chance must not rule and when he must decide carefully what he should do.

He stood back and, shielding his eyes, tried to follow the different paths against the mountainside. He went over in his mind the things the strange boy had said and tried to recall some gesture or sign that might give him a clue.

The right hand, he told himself finally. They would take the right-hand fork.

He was not sure. But somehow he remembered the sand-colored boy shifting his head in that direction, somehow he felt the Stone Towns lay the other way, on the left side. He turned that way and walked quickly. He wanted to put a number of twists and turns between himself and the conjurers before dark.

The path was steep and littered with rubble. It was

the correct path, he was more and more certain. And then all at once he was there, in the pass, among the tumble of stones and shattered boulders. In the saddle of the mountains the sun still shone and the yellow rock looked uglier than ever, in spite of the softening of shadows and coming dusk.

The Stone Towns. No wonder they were called that, for the world was stone here, the walls of the mountain, the cliffs above, the road below, the houses themselves. Ree climbed among the scree and over the broken slabs. He could make out the ruins of houses, walls with a blank door or window, a chimney, or even half a house, or one with no more damage than a caved-in roof.

The slanting light of sunset made it all eerier and more melancholy than it would be at noon, he thought. At noon he would not be able to see the ghosts. Now he could see them everywhere, the sad dim figures of the people who once lived here, leaning from the doors, moving like snakes from shadow to shadow, fluttering like birds inside the walls.

They were not ghosts, he knew. He was not afraid of them, not really. A little maybe, but mostly made desolate because they reminded him that he too had no home of his own, no place to live a real life, and no place to go except in his mind to return to the happiness of what once had been.

Something slid past a door which was no ghost. He

saw its high shoulders in gray fur and its huge jaws. Hanhan dogs. Naturally this was a neighborhood they would seek out and take over.

A pack of them then. He remembered how many had barked before the earthquake started. They must have sensed it in a way humans couldn't. There had been a lot of them. They were cowards—but a pack at night, and one lone sleeping boy . . .

He would find a house with some roof still left to it and sleep on the roof. And he would have to hurry. He walked along the rough street and finally discovered what he needed, a small house where part of the roof had collapsed inside it, so no stones were left leaning against the remaining portion, to make a ramp for hanhans or anyone else.

It was hard to clamber up, but Ree was glad. Hard for Ree, harder for dogs.

He squatted on the roof and stared out over the dusky valley. He could hear the sounds of running feet every now and then and the yipping-yelping of their voices, and once one stood below and panted for a few minutes, sniffing and smelling.

At first Ree thought he could not sleep. He was thirsty and hungry and worried, about the dogs a little, about another earthquake and perhaps about the ghosts. But he was tired, his legs ached from the day's climb. He pulled his blanket around him, and when next he opened his eyes, he knew it was well past midnight.

The sky was heavy with clouds; there were no stars, a little moon shone dimly for a moment in a rift. The hanhan dogs barked. One by one they raised their voices in the night and uttered that long maniacal chuckle: Hanhanhanhahahaha! They were close to him. What were they up to?

He moved over to the edge of the roof and looked down the street. Only a few houses away he could see them, a darker patch in the darkness. All of them gathered round one house. All taking turns at filling the air with their uncanny laughter. A strange thing for creatures to do, but then were not hanhan dogs strange creatures?

He listened for a little and suddenly, unable to bear it any longer, shouted as loudly as he could.

"Shut up, chitter-brains! Take yourselves off!"

The hanhans whirled in panic for a moment and then stopped, silent. He could feel them all staring at him; he could see a faint glow from the eyes of one or two. He drew a breath and was going to shout again.

And then from inside the house rose one more long trill of laughter—as shrill, as mad, as nerve-grating as the hanhan dogs. But Ree knew the voice was human.

5

REE CROUCHED at the roof's
edge, stiff with fear. There were ghosts then! Some
dead man's spirit lingered in that house and in the
darkness howled with laughter at the curious thing
that had befallen him. Some shadowy being mocked
the hanhan dogs, turning their living cries into this in-
side-out kind of weeping. Ree could not move. The
dogs stepped slowly away down the streets.

No, he was wrong! He was being foolish. Whatever
was inside that house was human and alive and that
was why the hanhans had crowded round, trying to
get in. They would not have been interested in a ghost.
They might have been afraid of it.

He must help this other person. He did not know
what to do. If he climbed down from his roof, the pack

might come after him. He had had enough trouble climbing up, in daylight and in no hurry. Whoever it was in the house must be safe, at least for a while. Ree did not intend that anyone else should see him while it was dark. He meant to keep his secret, he repeated to himself. Forever.

The sky was growing light in the east. Soon enough he could climb down to find out who was there, and why, and what could be done for him.

He drew back from the roof's edge. He was glad he had chosen to sleep here, in the open, and yet safe from the dogs and from the—ghosts. From most things. In his blanket he sat hunched and patient, waiting for the sun.

He was too thirsty and hungry to sleep anyway. The air was still and cold and smelled of dust, the clouds moved slowly overhead.

No further sounds came from the other house. The sun rose in mist and touched the rim of the mountains on each side of the pass with a troubled light. Ree thought that if he turned his head he might now see the High Plains, taller and prouder and far more beautiful than these mountains, but he did not look. Instead he lowered himself to the street and stood folding his blanket, staring around.

He hoped to see a spring or well, but there was none. He was ravenous and the food he had with him was so dry and hard he knew he could not chew and swallow it without water. And here there seemed to be no sign of gardens or fruit trees or any other thing. What had these people eaten in the days when they had lived here? Perhaps they survived on pebbles and drank dust and perhaps he must learn to do the same.

He looped his blanket over a shoulder and went slowly along the street. He was not sure which house the pack of hanhans had besieged. He glanced into one house and saw nothing, nor in the next. But at the third house he stopped. Half of it was empty shell, the roof gone. The other half still had a roof—and stones had been piled up and shoved about to make a new wall, a house that was half an old one. He saw no windows or door or other entry.

Ree walked around it. In the wall away from the street a small window had been barricaded from the inside, stuffed with various materials. This was the house, this was the one. The "ghost" must still be in there.

Ree dragged a rock to the wall and stood on it so that he could push away the rubble and old vibon skins and bits of wood that filled the window space. There was a scuffling sound from inside and then once again the shrill laughter. Ree paused.

"Who is it?" he called. "Who is inside?"

There was no answer. No ghost could have been quieter. But it was not a ghost. Ree could hear it holding its breath. A ghost would have no breath to hold.

And Ree could feel, could really hear, whatever it was standing just beyond the barricaded window, could really hear it not breathing, waiting to see what would happen next.

He pulled away some more of the stuff blocking the opening, and then suddenly it all fell away, some of it inside, some of it outside the house.

Ree turned his face away from the cloud of dust that rose around him and then stared into the room. The little light did not allow him to see much. Something shadowy moved against the wall, and then suddenly with a wild clucking and clacking a scrawny hen flew by his head and out into the air.

Ree fell off the rock and stood shaking and frightened, watching it go limping away. A hen! A hen had made that mad unmirthful chuckle? No. It could not have been. The voice had been human. Something else was inside those walls, a man, he knew.

He waited for his heart to stop pounding and for the light to grow stronger, and then he climbed up and looked in once more.

A man, it *was* a man. Old, so thin and frail he was nearly transparent, like smoke. Only his eyes gleamed out of the dimness, lunatic and bright and fiercely alive.

"Who are you?" asked Ree, as boldly as he could. "Who are you? Why are you here?"

The old man glared on, without answering. He did not move from his place against the wall. Ree looked

around the little room. It was filthy and dank and stinking. A barrel stood in one corner and a basket in another. The floor was covered with feathers and drop-
pings and broken egg shells.

"Who are you?" Ree repeated. He waited and there
was no answer. Finally he climbed inside.

In the room he knew that the old man could see what
he was and how he was disfigured. But he could not
believe it mattered. His gleaming skin would mean no
more to the old man than it had to the frightened hen.

Something had to be done. Someone must help this
pathetic creature. Ree did not really know what to do.
He looked into the barrel and saw that an inch of green
water lay at the bottom, slimy and smelly.

"Where do you get water?" he asked. He needed
water badly himself and the man must need it too.
"Have you a well or a spring?"

The silent stare replied.

Ree picked up the barrel. There must be water. Even
the people of the Stone Towns must have had water.

"I will be back," he said and, clutching the barrel,
went out the window. He walked along the street, keeping an eye out for a well or a trail to a stream or spring.
There *must* be one. And there was. In a little sort of
court to one side of the street he found the well. But
there was no bucket or rope or any other device for
bringing the water to the surface. The inside of the well
was rough and stones made convenient handholds and

footholds. He could climb down and drink himself, but he did not know how he could manage to fill the barrel.

The descent was easier than he had imagined. His foot slipped as he was halfway down and he splashed into the well. It was only waist deep and though the water was skinned with dust he found it refreshing. He swept the dust aside and bent and drank and wiped the water from his mouth and felt better.

He clambered out again and the climb up was far harder than he had imagined it would be. He wished he could manage to fall up as he had fallen down. And in the cold morning air his wet clothes clung to him and made it awkward to pull himself up and out.

He stood shivering beside the well and then walked over to the nearest house and peered into the broken walls. Nothing useful remained inside, only an old vibon pelt. It was moth-eaten and thin. Nevertheless he thought it would serve.

He shook it out and laid it on the ground and cut it into the longest strips he could devise and tied them together and made a rope for the barrel.

The barrel, like Ree, went easily down into the well, but balanced badly and spilled nearly half its contents on the way up. Still the water was certainly better than what the old man had had and there was enough of it for now. Ree carried it back with some feeling of satisfaction.

The man sat just as he had left him. Ree wondered if

he knew what was going on at all. He offered water in his cupped hands and at last the old man took a sip or two.

"Who are you?" asked Ree once again. "Why are you here?"

The man looked at him directly then, as though he really heard, and for answer he laughed. Ree hated the wild harsh sound of that laughter. It was worse than weeping.

He took the old man's arm. "Come," he said. "Come outside. It's daylight and the dogs are gone. We will find a better place to stay and I will feed you till you are strong again. Come."

The man jerked away from him and his eyes shone with fear and even hate. And yet he laughed that maniac's laugh.

Ree said gently, "I mean you no harm. I only want to help."

He tried to meet the other man's look calmly and steadily. But he could not help asking one more time, "Who are you? Why are you here?"

After a little silence Ree turned away. The old man could not answer, he was sure. Even if he had known who he was and why he was here, the words to tell Ree those things had gone from him. All that had been left to him was that madman's laughter.

Ree went outside and took off his wet clothes and left them to dry over a broken wall. With his blanket around him he searched up a few bits of wood from the empty houses and built a fire. He mashed the last of the fruits and some of the bread that Mali had given him and made a kind of broth by heating some water in half a crock he had discovered in the ruins. He ate boiled roots and bread, and when his clothes were dry, he went back into the stinking room and offered the old man the broth.

He turned his head away, but when Ree pressed the food on him again and again, he finally swallowed a little. Ree ate the rest, for he was hungry.

"Perhaps the hen will come back," he said aloud.

Obviously eggs had been what the man had lived on for a long time. A few husks of grain showed where the hen had fed, and in among the litter Ree found the rotting bodies of two other hens.

The old man had been abandoned here, Ree was sure of it. Someone else had pushed those stones around to make a wall and provided the hens and the barrel of water. Someone who had left the Stone Towns and had not wished to make the extra effort to take the old one along.

"Who did this?" he exclaimed. "Who left you here this way?"

There was no answer. Ree moved around the room, clearing up the garbage as best he could. When he could no longer bear the dust and odors, he left through the window.

The day was nearly gone. He must make some sort of plans. He could not sleep in that ghastly place and yet he did not want to leave the old man alone with the hanhan dogs. This house was not so high as the one on the roof of which he had spent the night before. But it was high enough. The hanhans could not reach him.

He walked around it, making sure no rock or rubble would offer them a way up. Then he followed the street a long way as it wound down the other side of the mountain. He could see trees and undergrowth far below him, and there were a few patches of grass. The houses stopped as the grass began to grow thicker and hide the ugly color of the rocks. What a strange people, who seemed to like living only where the earth was bare and hideous. He wondered where they all were now and if they found living in forests and meadows hateful and if they longed for the sight of the bald and broken crags. As he longed to see the High Plains or the hearthfire of his own family, the little carts and Merma's face.

He would not think about such things, not now.

He looked around and noted that there would be food near here, perhaps a spring with better water and more easily obtained. Certainly some kind of herbs and roots to gather. Perhaps he could trap a bird or a rabbit, though like all the True Men he ate meat only when he must. Even at a feast the True Men did not eat flesh.

Still the madman in the Stone Towns might prefer

such food, and he should eat. Perhaps with proper nourishment his mind would come back to him.

Ree returned the way he had come. Inside the house he once more offered the man water and this time the man drank deeply. The last bit of bread Ree dipped in the water to soften it and put it in the old man's hand, but it fell to the floor unheeded.

Ree was angry—he could have eaten it himself—but he said nothing. He placed the barrel within reach of the madman.

"I am going now," Ree said slowly and distinctly. "I will put stones and a skin across the window, so that the dogs cannot enter. I will sleep on the roof to keep them away. Don't be afraid. I will help you."

He tried to get the old man to look at him when he spoke, but the glittering eyes shifted here and there.

Outside the dusk was quiet and sad. I will stay here, Ree told himself as he pulled the stone he had used for a step to reach the window away from the walls. I will stay here and look after this man and feed him until he is strong. He is not wanted by his own people as I am not wanted by mine. We are both outcasts truly. We are together and I will help him as I can.

On the roof he stared up into the dusty sky. Here even the sky was blurred and unlovely. It was a proper place for two such people as Ree and the lunatic old man. Tomorrow he would search for food and water and see if he might find the hen, though he supposed if she had not run too far away the hanhan dogs would catch her.

In the dark he woke and heard them running along the street. He stood up and suddenly dropped the blanket from his body so his bare arms and face glowed like a lantern, and yelled at them. They loped away barking excitedly, and Ree lay down with a feeling of satisfaction. For once his illness or whatever it was had served him well.

He slept without waking the rest of the night.

In the morning he took the skin from the window and went into the stuffy room. The old man lay slumped on his side. Ree knelt before him.

"Old man," he said. The man drew a long wavering breath but did not move or open his eyes. Ree waited. Time went by and went by and went by, but the man did not breathe again.

6

REE STOOD in the street and looked down it toward the grassy fields and the forest. He could not see them, but he knew they lay below him and he longed to set off in that direction. Instead he turned aside and began to climb toward the highest ridges above the pass. Along those crests the other Stone Towns perched like hawks' eyries. Those people who had fled from the towns in the pass had in all likelihood gone to those other towns.

Ree had again barricaded the window in the ruined house so that no animal might get in.

But he could not bring himself simply to walk away and leave the mad man in this stark tomb. And too a half-fearful, half-angry curiosity nagged at Ree. He wanted to know why the old man had been so callously treated. Surely someone owed him something more than abandoning him to hunger and fear. At least the people of the Stone Towns should know how he had died.

The road was steep. He saw no signs of people or of houses as he followed the trail. It grew wider and seemed more traveled, and still the landscape, small as it was, remained empty. Perhaps the Stone Towns had all tumbled into the valleys. He walked on, and then behind him he heard a noise of footsteps and turned his head.

Had the conjurers caught up with him? Surely not. It would have happened long before this if they had wanted him and had pursued him. They did not, after all, even know his secret.

He waited and soon two small hurrying figures appeared on the path below him. They climbed steadily and fast, he could hear the tearing sound of their labored breathing before they were in speaking distance.

A boy and girl, younger than Ree, stocky, broad-faced, rough-skinned. They looked as solemn and hard-working as the True Men's ponies. They carried bundles on their backs and they hurried, hurried, hurried. When he spoke, they both jumped, startled, and stared at him with disbelief.

"Are you from the Stone Towns?" he asked, though he knew the answer.

The girl nodded. "Yes," she responded. "Where are you from?"

"I come from the wide valley," he said, which was true if not true enough. "I am looking for the Stone Towns."

The two of them stood, panting. "Not far," the boy said. "A little way now. But we can't wait. Our father said for us not to waste time, but to get quickly back to the Towns."

The girl watched Ree curiously. "Are you alone?" she asked. "Aren't you afraid?"

"Of what?" he wanted to know.

"Of the dragons," they replied together.

"One was seen on this road only two days ago," the boy added. Ree said nothing. "There are no dragons," he wanted to say. But how could he say it? Suppose someone had said to him, "There is a boy among the True Men who, after the sun sets, glimmers like a torch from some flame in his blood and bones." He would not have believed that, yet it was so. Who was he to say there were no dragons?

"I have seen no dragons," he answered at last.

"Our father saw one and one was seen on the road two days ago," the boy said. "They came out of the earth when it shivered and split. They breathe fire and smoke. Our father was sure he saw one cross the road in the early morning."

"We have to hurry," the girl added.

56

See page 7

They began to walk again and Ree went with them. He would have liked to offer his help with the bundles, but the two of them appeared to be so strapped and tied into their baggage he did not really believe they could unfasten themselves. They went on without talking.

Ree said after a bit, "The people who lived in the pass, before the earthquake, did they move up along the crests with you?"

The girl nodded. "Some of them did," she told him. "Many of them died. A few went into the valleys."

"It is a very bad time for the people of the Stone Towns," the boy went on. "We have trouble getting enough to eat. And some are afraid to use this road, the easiest and shortest road down into the valley, since it runs through the pass. The quakes still go on."

"You used the road," Ree pointed out.

The boy said, "Yes, because it is shorter. Our father made us promise to hurry because he did not want us to be caught up by the quakes or eaten by the dragons."

"Look," cried the girl, pointing. "You can see the town. You can almost see our house."

Ree glanced ahead. As in the pass, the street ran between two crooked rows of small squat stone buildings. There were a few stunted trees, and weeds grew in scraggly patches along the roadside. But here again there were no fields or orchards or gardens.

Such an ugly place, Ree thought. And still these

people lived here and had lived here since all time began.

"Our mother will be glad we are back safely," said the boy solemnly. "And that we have brought so much with us."

"What have you brought?" asked Ree.

"Grain for the hens," replied the girl.

"And dried meat and fruits," her brother went on. "And cheese! But my father said we should not eat it till he came. We haven't had cheese in over a year."

"Where is your father then?" asked Ree.

The girl gestured down the mountainside, away from the wide valley. "He is coming. But he had to bring two goats with him and he is slow."

"Will you raise the goats here?" asked Ree, staring around him in wonder. Even goats could not subsist on these weeds and dry bushes.

The children looked at him curiously. "No, we only raise hens," the boy responded. "He will drive the goats into the wide valley in the next day or two. They are meant for the man who sent the vibon skins which we carried over the mountains."

They walked on and by and by were among the small houses.

"We live there," the boy said, nodding his head. "The third house past the well."

"May I have a drink?" asked Ree. He was very thirsty, and hungry too. Food he would not ask for, he could do without eating, but water he must have.

"Yes," the boy said. "We have good water here, the best in all the Stone Towns. And the well is deep, very deep, and never goes dry."

They did not stop and Ree went alone and hauled up a bucket full to the brim. The water was good indeed, clear and sweet, and he drank a great deal and then walked on.

In the road he found a bird's feather, soft blue and white. It was the only gentle or lovely thing he had encountered since he came into this country. He picked it up. It was the kind of thing he liked to take to Merma as a "present." He held it in his fingers a moment, before he let it drift once more down through the air.

The two children had reached their own doorway and a woman was helping them unstrap their bundles and lower them to the ground. She gave Ree a sharp glance.

"That's the boy we met on the trail," the girl explained. "He did not know about the dragons."

Ree went toward them. Should he simply tell the woman what he knew and then go? He thought not. He had traveled a long way on this errand. He would not go back without speaking to someone who had known the old man and might care that he was dead.

"Is there someone here who used to live in the Stone Towns in the pass?" he asked. "The ones the earthquake ruined?"

The woman still looked at him with hostility. "Yes,"

she answered. "There is a man in the house next door."

She turned back to the task of opening the packs. She is afraid I will ask for something to eat, Ree thought. He moved away. None of them spoke to him again.

"Good-bye," he said, but they did not seem to hear.

At the next house he knocked on the narrow wooden door, and when it opened, a man looked out. His wide face too was unsmiling and unwelcoming.

"What do you want?" he asked bluntly.

Ree hesitated. His mission seemed suddenly pointless and stupid.

"Your neighbor said you were one of those who left the Stone Towns in the pass during the earthquakes," he began.

The man's face darkened. "Anyone who stayed was a fool," he growled. "The ground opened and the houses tumbled in and people died. And it's still going on."

Ree waited a moment, and when the man did not continue he said, "Someone stayed, an old man by himself. He could not speak."

"Old Padran." The man nodded. "Once he could speak well enough. But he was ever strange. He used to say the rocks over the pass hated him and hurt his eyes. He wanted his wife and son to leave and go into the valley with him. And when they wouldn't, he tried to plant trees around the houses. Trees, to fall across the trail and drop leaves and branches and make keeping it clean harder than ever! He said trees helped him breathe when the dust was thick. Once he said he liked to hear the hanhan dogs. And when the ground broke open and his wife died and his son ran away and left him behind, he began to laugh like the dogs, all the time."

"He's dead," put in Ree. "He died in the night in one of the houses. I found him there and tried to get him to eat, but it was too late. He died."

"Many people died," the man said shortly. "Padran was no more immortal than the rest of them."

He did not look at Ree but past him, as though he saw his ugly little town and the street through the pass. There was something terribly troubled in his look, as though he had lost something but was not certain what it was.

Finally Ree asked, "Why was he left behind? Why didn't you bring him with you when you came here?"

The man turned his eyes toward Ree and gazed at him oddly.

"Why should we bring him with us? A man who was already half hanhan dog. Let him stay and laugh with them. We were in trouble enough and there was nothing to laugh about," the man responded angrily. "He was always a curse to himself and everybody else. And what affair is it of yours anyway?" He shut the door. Ree stood a minute and then he shouted, "He's dead. I thought someone should know!"

He walked away. The woman and the two children were still busy sorting the packages and sacks the children had brought home. They did not seem to see him, but as he started along the street the boy came running up behind him and said breathlessly, "Watch out for the dragons. They roam about in the early mornings especially. My mother said to tell you."

Ree said, "Thank you. And thank your mother."

The warning was kindly meant, however foolish. It touched Ree a little. Plainly no one was going to offer him anything to eat. The True Men always fed a stranger, even though it was the last dried fruit or bit of bread. Altogether the True Men led a different sort of life, not this strange stony existence where nothing seemed quite real. Yet the woman had been concerned for his safety and sent her child to urge him to beware.

He went on. When he was out of sight of the houses, he left the road and started down the slopes toward the forest.

The way was steep and rough, sometimes he slid along the rocks much faster than he had intended and landed harder. Still he was glad to leave the easier trail, for he had had enough of the Stone Towns. This country was no place for anyone raised in the warmth and color, the songs and bells and laughter of the True Men.

Yet the True Men were like the people of the Stone Towns in one way, he thought bitterly. He and Padran alike had been cast out because of strange things which had happened to them. It was surely harmless for the old man to think himself a hanhan dog. It was surely harmless that after dark Ree's skin shone like mica in the sun. For these things they had been condemned and exiled. There was something wrong about it.

It was growing shadowy. He had hoped to travel longer, but now he must stop. He would find a hiding place, though he did not think he could be seen by anyone had he slept in the open. And he had learned that the hanhan dogs, however many, were afraid of his glowing shape. Nevertheless he found a concealing shelter of overhanging rock and prepared to spend the night there.

He was glad of his blanket. The afternoon had been pleasant in the sun, almost warm, but the night was cold. He did not expect to sleep for he was very hungry and the rocks on which he lay were hard and chill. He huddled in his blanket and stared into the dark.

For the first time in his life he had left behind the High Plains and the wide valley. When the sun rose in the morning, he would be looking at landscape entirely new to him—in every direction.

He would perhaps never see the High Plains again.

In spite of all his efforts he could not keep that old life out of his mind. He thought of hearthfires and the smell of bread baking, the shadows of the moving carts. They would all be asleep now, Ginda and Mali and Fadan and Merma, asleep by the low fire. Only Ree would be missing.

Yet even if he were with them in the wide valley, he would not be there. He would be sleeping apart and hidden from them.

He would not quite be one of them. He would be a presence maybe worrisome to his family and friends.

Perhaps they were right then, the people of the Stone Towns and the True Men.

Perhaps those who were unlike their fellows should be sent away or even abandoned and allowed to die, like Padran.

Perhaps in time of trouble such people truly made trouble worse.

It was a hurtful thought and kept him awake for many hours. He slept at last, and when he woke, the morning was raw and faintly misty.

Outside his stone shelter squatted a dragon and from its mouth licked red flames and clouds of smoke.

7

REE LAY quietly watching. The dragon was not large, only half again his own length, and its eyes were dull and filmed. It did not seem to see him.

It squatted motionless on big bowed legs and then he saw its brown-and-green scaled sides fall in across its ribs in a slow breath. Once again the long scarlet tongue flickered out of its mouth and in the frosty air its moist breath condensed into puffs of smoky mist.

Ree stood up slowly and went toward it. It must be nearly dead of cold. He knew what it was—a nugano, he had heard of them. Much like the tiny dobels which basked on stones and logs on the High Plains, eating ants and flies. The same kind of creature only grown a hundred times larger, but no more harmful and no more a dragon.

What was it doing so far from its home? Nuganos lived close to big bodies of water—lakes or rivers. That was why there was none of them in the wide valley where the springs and pools were not ample for them.

The long flame of tongue shot out, and the white fog from its lungs. No wonder the people of the Stone Towns were frightened. Nuganos had surely never been seen anywhere near here before. Perhaps the earthquakes had indeed released them from some cave far underground. More likely those fierce tremors had thrown them into panic and this one had run the wrong way, up the mountain and away from its home.

Ree pitied it. There was nothing for it to eat here and no water and little shelter from the sun. He touched it cautiously with his hand and felt the cool scaly skin. He could feel the slow pulse of its cold blood. A creature as different from himself as day from night.

He shoved and pushed until the beast turned and walked a few awkward steps down the mountain ahead of him. He saw that it would be a hard thing to do, but he had made up his mind. He would take this nugano down the mountain, back into the rich and dripping forest where it belonged, where no one would think it strange and terrible and evil.

After an hour he was ready to abandon his idea. He had to take a back-and-forth course to find a descent that the big reptile could manage. He had to push and shove and guide with his foot and watch out that the nugano did not turn and snap at him with its crushing jaws.

But soon the task grew easier, the animal seemed to realize that it was going home. Or perhaps as the day warmed it simply became less sluggish. It went faster and faster and found the most convenient way for itself once or twice and didn't have to be prodded forward. And when the bare rocks gave way to smoother mossy stones and patches of grass and shrubby bushes, it kept ahead of Ree all the time, lumbering along eagerly on its short bent legs in a way that made him smile. He wished Merma could see it.

When he came on a path through the low woods, he followed it and left the nugano to fend for itself, which it certainly seemed able to do. He could hear it scuffling away through the undergrowth purposefully. It was going home.

Home. The path led somewhere. Someone used it and Ree hoped to find along it some place where he might ask for bread. He did not hope to meet someone who, like the True Men, would offer a meal to any stranger any time. But perhaps he could barter an afternoon's work for food, as the people of the Stone Towns did. Or he might even come on some plant he recognized and might dig it up and eat.

Probably not. This country was as unlike the High

Plains and the wide valley as was the country of the Stone Towns. It was stony and sloping. But the earth was rich and the plants that grew from it were lush and the flowers brightly colored.

Why had not Padran left the Stone Towns and come here to live? Ree wondered. Why had he not left the yellow rocks he hated and come to live in this pleasant place? Ree thought he knew the answer.

The trees around him were small and scattered and he did not recognize them. They were misted with buds and tiny new leaves. In the light of midday they seemed made of light, they seemed like silvery-green clouds ready to float away.

The grass underfoot was thick and soft and the path wound cleanly through it, firm and well defined. He saw flowers which he did not know, and one or two which he had seen before, and a bush covered with white blooms and crawling through it a vine with scarlet trumpet-shaped flowers. Had he not been so tired and hungry he might have admired it more, but as it was he could only wonder if the white blossoms would ever become fruit and if the scarlet vine sprang from a tuber worth digging and eating.

He stumbled on and saw a house and a garden and a woman working in among the rows of vegetables, all at once, as though he had rounded a curve and come on them without warning. But he knew that was not so, he had simply been going along so occupied with his own misery that he had not noticed the little farm until he was almost on it.

He quickened his pace. He thought the woman would look up when she heard his footsteps, but she did not and went on carefully setting her slips of plants into the brown earth and covering the roots with swift gentle pats.

He stood waiting, and when she had settled the last little sprout into the row, she raised her head and smiled.

"I had to get them all in the ground," she said. "They should have been started ten days ago. The winter's been hard and I was afraid of a late frost."

She stood up and wiped her hands on her clothes, which were already muddy enough.

"I think they'll be all right," she added. "I heard the bellbird sing this morning. I've never known there to be a frost after the bellbird sang."

Then she frowned and looked about her. "But I've still got so much to do. So much. And I haven't been up the hill to see if my fruit trees are in bloom. Or found where my brown hen has her nest. Or—" She stopped talking and stared at Ree.

"You are one of the True Men," she said finally. "I'm sure of it, though I never saw a boy before, only grown men and women. They have come this way on occasion. What are you doing here?"

What am I doing here? Ree wanted to repeat. Instead he answered, "I have been traveling and I am hungry. I'll be glad to help with your work for a little bread or some boiled roots."

The woman said, "Look, there's the first greening beetle I've seen this year. They'll eat my cabbages." She reached out a hand and snatched at the beetle as it zoomed by. "Did you ever see such a color? When the light catches the wings, it's almost gold, not green."

Ree watched the beetle whirring away. "Just a little bread," he said again. "I am a good worker. I could do whatever you want."

"Oh, I can give you bread," the woman answered. "I have two new loaves I baked yesterday. And we can have an egg or two and some roots. They are left over from last fall, and a little withered, but they are good enough."

She washed her hands and face at a well by the house door and so did Ree, and he drank again. He sat outside and waited, for she did not ask him in, but soon she brought out a big dish of boiled roots and some eggs in a pan and the new bread.

Ree tried not to eat more than his share, but he was hugely hungry and he had not tasted anything so good in a long while.

"Eat," the woman urged, and walked over to a bush to see if it was in bud, poked among the grass to find some bulbs coming up, shaded her eyes to watch a flock of birds.

"There they come, there they come!" she called. "The blue-throated soarers. They come every year when my fruit trees bloom and nest close by and keep the caterpillars away."

Ree recognized them. The True Men too welcomed the bellbirds and the soarers. He wondered what kind of fruit she grew.

"There's plenty of food," she called out. "Have all you want. I have more than enough. By the time the leaves on my goldentongue bush are as long as my finger, my hens will be laying better than ever and I'll have much from the garden, greens and peas and such."

She came back to stand beside him and eat a piece of bread. "Do you live here all alone?" asked Ree, for he did not want to give her space to remember that he had not answered her question.

"Yes," she nodded. "I've lived alone here seventeen years now. Once my family lived here with me and there were many farms close at hand. But there was a sickness, half the people died, all my family except my sister and her husband and little girl. The sickness went on for two years. So people moved away, one by one. The farms fell into ruin. My sister and her husband went too, and finally I was the only one left."

Ree was startled. Had this woman been abandoned then, like Padran?

"Why did you not go with them?" he asked.

The woman looked at him earnestly. "I couldn't,"

she said at last. "My sister thought I should go and so did her husband and the others. But it was spring, you know, and the garden had to be tended. I was waiting to hear the bellbirds, to be sure the frost was gone. I thought I would wait till the goldentongue bush bloomed and then I would go. But when it bloomed, so many things in the garden needed care, and I had my hens. And the blue lilies in the woods were about to flower. I wanted to see them. I wanted to see if the cufflebirds under the eaves had four little ones or three."

She smiled. "Last year they had four. You can see the bits of the nest up there. They'll throw it all away before they start the new one."

"And you and your sister have never seen each other since?" Ree wanted to know.

She shook her head. "At first she sent messages that I should come and see her and her other children and visit for a while, even if I didn't want to stay and live there. I always said I would come. I wanted to go. I always meant to go. It's a long journey though. Every time I got ready to leave, I would think about all the things that would have happened while I was away. I'd think about my cupflowers blooming without anyone to see them. And how the cufflebirds might fledge while I was away. Or how—" she broke off. "I have never gone," she finished quietly. "There are many things to take care of here."

Ree ate the rest of the eggs thoughtfully. "I could stay here and care for all your hens and your fruit trees and your garden while you went."

She burst out laughing. "You could not be my eyes and ears," she answered. "You could not see the blue lilies as I would see them or hear the tikers singing under the hearthstone. You might feed my little brown hen and find her nest, but you could not feel for me how warm and round her eggs are or watch how she tilts her head when I come out to scatter grain on a cold day."

"That is true," Ree agreed and smiled. In fact there was nothing he could do for her. He could not even help her in order to show his gratitude for the food. Whatever he might offer to do would be something she might rather do herself. Still he repeated, "I will gladly work for you, because you gave me the food. Is there something I can do?"

She shook her head. "No, it isn't really work, you see, it is just what I do." She looked somewhat puzzled. "It is just what I *am*," she added.

Ree got up. "Then I will be gone," he said. "It was kind of you to give me food. I am in your debt."

"No," she replied. "There's food here always. I will not do without because I fed you. Where will you go?"

Ree hesitated. "Toward the lake," he answered. He looked down toward the dark forest. Those trees grew along the river which ran into the lake, he knew that.

The lake was vast. All sorts of people lived around it. The woman needn't know more about his destination, since he did not know more himself. She took his arm.

"Then you *can* do something for me," she said. "My sister has her home close to the point where the river runs into the lake. Her husband is a weaver, now, I've heard. Her name is Renka. I am Brada. Try to find her and give her a message from me. Say that— say that I will come, in a few years, when there is not so much to do here."

"Very well," Ree promised. "I will remember. Renka, the weaver's wife."

The woman looked at once sad and pleased. She released his arm. He set out, following the path that led downhill from her door. When he was well past the garden, he turned and called, "Thank you. And goodbye." For a moment there was no response, and then she called back softly, "Listen! The bellbird is singing again . . ."

The sun was low in the sky by the time he reached the forest's edge. He walked more and more slowly as he approached. He had not seen anything like this before. It was exciting and awesome, he was more than a little bit afraid. Such monsters of trees, towering up into the evening air. Such a thick sky of leaves far overhead, surrounding the great trunks, some smooth, some gnarled, some barbed or pitted. Inside, birds called back and forth, their voices were sharp and harsh. Under the trees shadows slipped and sidled—who could say whether something walked there or did not?

Ree backed away. It was so strange a place, and dark. Even in daylight it would be dim. He would have to go very carefully through that green dusk. He would not follow any path, he would walk where he would not be likely to meet another human. Anyone who saw him in that jungle would know his secret.

Now he retraced his steps and found a hollow among tall grasses where he could sleep. It was warm and he hated covering himself with his blanket. In the night he woke and found, to his horror, that he had thrown the blanket aside. Hastily he huddled under it again. He did not suppose anyone would come this way, certainly not at this hour. But he was alarmed and lay awake for a long time, and from the forest came sounds he had not heard before, howls and screams and hoots, spine-chilling in the blackness. He wondered whether he should go on. Perhaps there was some other road he could take to—to where?

Where was he going and why was he going there? He held up his hand and watched its glow against the sky. No brighter—and no dimmer—than when he had left the True Men in the wide valley.

What was this thing and why had it happened to

him? He was Ree, the arrow-swift, the arrow-straight; one of the True Men, born on the High Plains. He had loved that life, the songs and the rich flat green fields of summer, the bells and campfires of winter. And what was he now, with no life and no name, cowering among the rocks and grasses like a nugano? What should he do with himself for the rest of his days? Was there not to be a place for him ever again? He pulled his arm back under the blanket. Tomorrow he would find Renka, the weaver's wife. That was a debt he would pay. And after that he would—he would go into the lake and wash and wash and wash, until his skin dissolved away, sloughed off, disappeared. And then he would wash his flesh away, past veins and muscles and sinews, down to his bare bones, if necessary. He would—he shut his eyes and shut his heart, so that nothing could get in, and drifted back to sleep.

IN THE morning the day was overcast, the clouds were threatening and somber. He ate the rest of the bread Brada had given him and some leaves and shoots which seemed wholesome, and at last made his way inside the forest.

The undergrowth was thinner than he had imagined it would be, waist-high ferns and ropy creeping vines and an occasional weedy bush or small tree, struggling for light, not like the wall of foliage and branches along the margin of the jungle. But the leaves overhead grew denser and shut out the day almost completely. Noisy birds called back and forth. The sounds were screeches and squawks, but they were gentler and less alarming than the night noises had been. Birds were not all that lived here however—where the ground was soft he found hoofprints of several kinds and the marks of a big claw-sheathed paw.

There was, after all, no path to follow or avoid. He had only his sense of direction to guide him.

After every few steps he stopped and glanced around. Nothing pursued him. Once he heard a squeal and slither in the ferns but nothing more. He began to hurry. He would like to be out of this place before dusk. How would he know it was dusk, among these shadows? Noon would never be bright here. He walked and walked and was afraid that he was lost. He would have to spend the night here after all. The light grew fainter and fainter.

Where would he sleep, to be safe from all those things he had heard shrieking and yowling last night? Would those things, like the hanhans, be afraid of his shining skin? Once he heard a rumble of thunder, he was almost certain. But not quite. In such a place might there not live some beast whose bellow was like thunder?

He grew more and more afraid. Not even in dreams had he known such enormous trees existed, or such air, so heavy, so ominous. He might crouch among the ferns and vines, but unimagined horrors might crouch there with him. He might climb one of those vast trunks and cling among its branches, but who knew what might be aloft there with him? Just above **his** head or gliding toward his grasping hands?

His heart raced and every falling leaf made him start.

He stood still at last in the twilight and made himself breathe quietly and waited for his heart to cease quivering. There was no need to be afraid. He was a boy without a home, without a life. Had he not half-promised to drown himself in the river? Why should he fear the beasts, or worse, that lived here?

He sank to the ground and did not trouble to cover himself but lay on the damp bare earth. All night as in a fever he heard the sounds of creatures, of monsters, their padding feet, their snarls and yells, their bodies crashing through the ferns. Before daylight something would kill him, with teeth or claws, with suffocating coils or burning poison. He did not care.

Only toward morning he became aware suddenly of a faint steady noise, something he had not noticed before, strange yet pleasant. It must be, he told himself. The river! It must be. And so close!

He wanted suddenly and most terribly to see it. He longed with all his being to see it and touch it and taste it. Perhaps he could indeed be cured by its water. Certainly he had to see it.

Stealthily he reached out for his blanket and pulled it around him. If he could hide for the next hour, perhaps he would manage to stay alive and reach the river.

He couldn't wait. The hour was too slow, too long; he picked himself up and with his blanket around him began to walk toward the sound. He held his hands in front of him and by their faint radiance he made his way. He was aware of what a sight he made—and what an easy target. It would be odd if he had lain all night for the killers to see and been unmolested; and now that he had decided not to die they should find him.

Nothing found him. He went stumbling on. For a little space the jungle grew quiet and then the day noises began, and the sound of the river grew louder and suddenly there it was! Deep and green and lapping pleasantly against its banks and swirling over a small rock ledge to make the steady murmur he had recognized in the dark.

The river was wide, mist hovered above it and he could not see the other side. He walked down the bank and thrust his hand into the water. Nothing happened. His hand gleamed like a fish below the surface. He put his other hand in and rubbed them together, watching them twist and turn beneath the ripples.

Finally he took off all his clothes and slipped into the cool water. From the river bed he gathered sand and scoured his skin the way he might wash a dirty shirt and let the current, strong and eager, rinse the sand away. Once he thought he had succeeded, had really rubbed out the glow, but then he realized that full daylight had come, putting out the strange light of his own body, as always, as it put out the stars or foxfire.

He lay in the water a few minutes longer and then he emerged and put his shirt and trousers back on. It had been silly to think such a thing. Whatever it was, he would not be rid of it, ever. He would not know ever again what it was like to be as others were and walk as others walk. Chance ruled the True Men and they accepted its ruling.

Under his clothes his body was damp, and the drops of water clung to him and did not dry away, for the air was still and heavy with moisture and hot. The clouds swam slowly over, they seemed hardly higher than the tops of the great trees. Ree followed the river, which moved beside him tirelessly, as his little pony had once done. Sometimes it spoke in a cool and musical voice, liplapping along the sandy shore, and sometimes it clattered and roared, as a wind lifted suddenly and then fell.

There would be rain soon, Ree knew. A storm perhaps, the day was so oppressive and threatening. The clouds went overhead sullenly, he could almost hear them grate against one another. The little squalls rushed down the river. Once again he heard thunder.

Ree halted and gazed around. Surely people lived somewhere near. He saw no sign of any other living being. He wondered if the houses were not back behind the line of greenery along the edge of the forest. There was no path among the coarse grass and scattered bushes growing on the riverbank. He would have to wait out the storm under some natural cover, which was likely just as well, he told himself, and was surprised a few minutes later to look up and find that there were houses ahead of him, little low thatched houses blending into the ground and the undergrowth so that they were hard to see.

He watched as he passed them by and still saw no one. Were the houses deserted or the people still sleeping? It was mysterious.

A streak of lightning cut the sky from clouds to earth and the sound of that tearing followed almost immediately, rippling toward him and then falling gigantically on his ears and all around him, shaking the ground like the earthquake, and frightening him.

But then it rolled away, booming and banging into the distance, and the first drops of rain came quickly, whispering down here and there. The wind began to blow fiercely and sent sand rasping against his shins.

He was accustomed to storms, he was often out in them, winter and summer. He knew how to protect himself. The rain increased, the wind blew more strongly, swinging suddenly to another direction. The sand spurted into his face. He turned toward the forest and ran to reach the shelter of a little copse growing close to it. A bolt of lightning struck into the jungle just ahead of him, he threw his arms across his eyes, dazzled. And when he opened his eyes he could not be sure where he was—the rain was so heavy he thought he must be drowning. Should he fall into the river, he would not know it, for the land was like a river. The wind flung him this way and that, the world trembled under the thunder claps.

He gasped and staggered on, holding his hands over his forehead to shield his eyes so that he might see well enough to get his bearings. He had not known there were such storms, the whole winter's storms in the wide valley rolled into one were not so brutal as this. He was afraid to stop for fear of being killed by the slash of wind and rain and afraid to go on for fear of almost everything.

The wind shoved him forward and then suddenly was slamming at his chest, so that he reeled backward. His blanket was sodden and its weight pulled at his shoulders. The gale swerved again and beat against the side of his head and face, filling his ear with water, and he had to go where he was blown. He fell over a bush and screamed in panic, and picked himself up and was thrown down again.

He reached out and felt for the bush and found it and held on, and when the wind eased a very little, he managed to struggle to his feet and stumble away.

He was certain the storm was going to kill him, but he could not let himself huddle on the ground and die. The air screamed as it gusted around him, this way and that, and he wanted to scream defiantly back, but had no breath. The sky was almost black when he glimpsed it and he twice heard the great jungle trees splinter and crack.

He was close to the forest, he should try to get in among the trees and perhaps there he would find some refuge. He groped along and touched something, brushed against it and thought it must be the thick outer wall of the forest. His wet hands pushed against the twigs and leaves. And then he realized what it was, one of the little thatched houses.

He leaned against it, gasping and crying, and the gale drove him suddenly sidewise and he clawed at the house and tried frantically to cling to the thatch. And suddenly something grabbed him and pulled him, a man's voice shouted, "Quickly, quickly, inside! For the love of your life, inside!"

Ree could not resist, did not have the strength to resist, even had he wanted to. He fell through the opening and lay on the floor and heard the man grunt and pant as he fought to close the door.

There was a snecking noise and the sounds of the storm went farther away and Ree could catch his breath. The wind still howled, the rain flooded down, but in the house there was a little shell of quiet and stillness to keep the tumult away, and Ree lay inside that shell, almost fainting, while the water drained away from him and the raging weather in his head died down.

After a while he sat up dizzily. It was almost completely dark in the hut. There was no fire, no torch, no gleam of daylight. Only where Ree sat the bright aura of his own being showed him the bare interior of the little house and the man moving about in the dimness near what appeared to be a small hearth with a cooking pot. He waited for the man to speak, to shout at him and order him out into the tempest. Or to scream in fright and disgust.

But nothing happened. The man went on with his task, whatever it was. Ree wondered what kind of man it would be who could accept him so equably and not even turn to stare.

Gradually the roar of the wind died away, and though the rain still beat upon the thatch, it grew much quieter in the little house. The man spoke.

"You must be a stranger here," he said suddenly. "None of us River Dwellers would have gone out this day. We could smell that storm coming three days ago."

Ree nodded. The man waited and then said, "Speak, stranger, if you are there. I am blind, you know."

Ree almost cried out. He was safe!

"No, I did not know," he replied. "Yes, I am a stranger. I too knew the storm was coming, but I did not know it would be so terrible. I did not know how to hide from it." He paused. "How did you know I was outside? I am grateful for your help. I would have died."

"I heard your hands on my walls and door," the

blind man answered. "My hearing is keener than most. I can tell the sound of a boy's hands from the rattle of branches or sand against my walls. And who would not open a door and save another man from the storm? For the storms here are killers indeed."

Ree got up and moved a little closer. He could see now that the man was combing and carding vibon hair and a spindle stood by the hearth. A blind man could spin as well as any, perhaps better.

"But those of us who live along the river know when they are coming and we seal our chimneys and bar our doors and stay inside," the man went on. "Our houses are stout, though you might not believe so." He laughed. "Some of us think that in appearance they are so like the earth and the jungle scrub that the storm cannot see them. That's nonsense, of course. It is because they are sturdy and shaped into the ground so that the wind goes easily over and around them. My father's father built this hut and it has withstood far worse storms than this one."

"I understand," Ree answered, not certain that he did but wanting the man to know he was listening. There was a little space and the man's hands dragged the comb through the wool and his fingers patted to see if it was clean and straight.

"Do you live here alone?" asked Ree. It was all he could think to say. He was still exhausted from his battle with the rain and wind and still stunned with relief that the man could not see. What a terrible thing, to be glad of someone else's misfortune! He was ashamed and yet he could not help it.

"Yes," the man answered, "if you mean alone in this house. I have friends and relatives who live nearby. They are kind to me, although I do not for the most part need their help. I can do for myself most things. And the things I cannot do, I do without."

He laughed again and went on with his work. Then he said, "The rain will slacken soon. I'll unseal the chimney then and make a fire. You must be very wet. We'll have some food too."

"Thank you," answered Ree.

They sat on while the blind man's hands worked slowly and smoothly away and the rain fell steadily on the roof. Ree almost dropped to sleep.

Suddenly the blind man raised his head. "Someone is coming," he said. Ree strained but he heard nothing. The man must be imagining things. Why would anyone be out in such weather? And then he thought he did indeed hear something.

He jumped to his feet. What could he do? Crawl under his dripping blanket? Hide behind the rough cot or the low chest in the corner? What could he do?

The knock on the door echoed loud in the tiny room. The blind man put down the wool and the card and stood up.

"Wi—will you open the door?" asked Ree hesitantly.

"Certainly," he answered. "I always open my door. A blind man learns to trust. If he begins to doubt one person, he must soon doubt all."

He paused thoughtfully. The knock sounded again. "Did I not open my door to you?"

"No, wait!" Ree cried. "The storm is gone! It is dark now, it is night."

"Night!" cried the blind man. "What can night mean to me?"

He stepped slowly across the room and opened the door.

"Come in, friend," he said evenly. "Come in from the rain."

Ree stood staring, helpless. And into the circle of light that fell shining from Ree, the arrow, born on the High Plains, moved the wet figure of the sand-colored boy's father.

The conjurer!

9

SHOCK, terror, greed and crafty delight—these things Ree saw plainly, one after another, in the conjurer's face. For just a breath he had looked disbelieving, such a creature could not be real, could not be alive. And then all those other emotions had swiftly followed in the sand-colored eyes. But when he spoke, his voice betrayed none of them. It was soft and even and monotonous, like his sand-colored skin and hair.

"Good evening, Andara," he said. "Do you remember me? Tarem, the healer and magician?"

"I remember you," the blind man answered. "Is there something you want?" He was not impolite, but Ree understood at once that Andara knew Tarem would come to his door only because the conjurer was in need of something.

"The storm," explained Tarem. "A bit of the roof blew off our cart and the tinder got wet. Might I borrow some tinder to start a new fire?"

"Of course," Andara replied. "It's time for me to start a fire, anyway. I have a visitor. Caught in the storm and lucky not to be killed."

He moved in his sure unhurried fashion to the hearth and pulled a wooden bung, padded with cloth, from the chimney. A shower of damp soot came with it. Then the blind man picked up a box and opened it and held it out in the general direction of the conjurer.

"Here," he said. "Help yourself. I've plenty."

Tarem scooped up some of the dry stuff in his hand and slipped it into a leather sack. His eyes never moved from Ree's face.

"Have you dry wood for a fire?" asked Andara.

"A little," answered Tarem.

"Then I expect your wife will be waiting to start supper," the blind man continued.

The conjurer scowled. He did not like being thus courteously asked to leave. He looked Ree up and down with care, weighing what he saw.

"I suppose she will," he said finally. "We are grateful for the tinder."

"You are welcome," answered Andara.

The sand-colored man backed out the door, his eyes still fixed on Ree. He shut the door reluctantly. Andara piled wood on the hearth, added a little heap of tinder and struck a spark from two rough stones. He sat close to the fire, waiting to be sure it was burning well. Ree feared for him, but the man seemed to know just what he was doing. Soon there was a real blaze on the hearth stones, and Andara swung the cooking pot over the fire.

Ree's blanket steamed in the heat. It was airless and almost too hot in the house, but Ree was certainly not willing to have the door opened. Anyway, the rain still fell, the wind still occasionally blew over the thatched roof with a shrill sound.

They ate without speaking and when they were done Andara placed the bowls in the empty pot and set them outside the door, opening and shutting it quickly.

"The weather will clean them well," he said approvingly. "Usually I must scour them out with sand and then wash them. It isn't a hard task, but somehow it always pleases me to have the rain and wind do it for me. Those two things cause me much trouble, it is only fit that they should save me a little once in a while."

"Yes," answered Ree, knowing the man could not see his smile, for it seemed to him too an agreeable thought.

Andara carefully pushed ashes over the fire until it was only a glow, no brighter, perhaps not so bright as the glow that fell from Ree's bare face and arms.

"I have a dry blanket for you to sleep on, but nothing else," Andara said. "I do not have many guests."

"I will be glad of the blanket," answered Ree. "I am not accustomed to more."

He took the blanket and lay down on it in a corner of the room, away from the fire. Andara by and by lay down on his cot. Ree listened to his breathing growing strong and deep and regular as he fell asleep. Ree would not sleep himself. In a little he would get up and find his own blanket and slip out into the stormy night. Tarem's look had left no doubt of his plans for this magic creature, this boy who shimmered in the gloom like a pale moon in a cloudy sky, and already the wheeled cage would be waiting for something better than a two-headed goat.

Ree must be up in the night and gone as quickly as he could. He could not linger here. Andara need not know when he was going or why. He did not wish to impose further on Andara's hospitality. And he did not wish Andara to know why Tarem frightened him or to be involved any more than he was.

The rain fell softly, softly, and when he opened his eyes, the door to the house stood open and sun fell through it and it was morning. Andara sat by the hearth, and when Ree stirred on his blanket, he said cheerfully, "Good morning. I hope you slept well."

Ree was frightened. He had supposed he would be safe in daylight, always, but now it was not so, now he was not safe anywhere, day or night. And he had missed his best chance for escape. Tarem would seize him as soon as he stepped outside.

"There is bread here, and some dove fruit," went on Andara. "I find that makes a fine breakfast."

Ree still lay, watching the door in panic. Tarem would not come in the house for him, he knew. But he could not stay here longer. And once he left Andara's hut—Tarem would find him.

Andara spoke again, in a voice suddenly grave and solemn. "I am sorry that I opened the door to Tarem. I did not know you feared him. He is harmless, all his charms are powerless. I know him well. Years ago he came often to try to persuade me to trade my vibon hair for his silly lotions, to give me back my sight."

He laughed. "I was born blind. How could he give me back what I have never had? Likely now that I have gone so long without it I would not know what to do with it if I had it. Anyway my mother and father tried all those useless remedies when I was a baby."

"How did you know I was afraid of Tarem?" asked Ree.

"I can tell such things," the blind man answered. "I can hear and smell fear, as you cannot."

"It is not Tarem's amulets and charms which frighten me," said Ree, but he did not go on. In the first place there was no way to explain to Andara what was strange about him that made him so valuable to Tarem. In the second place there was no need to worry the blind man with his troubles, or make him feel guilty about revealing Ree's secret to Tarem.

He stood up and helped himself to the bread and dove fruit. It was a good breakfast, in truth.

"Is there something I can do for you?" he asked suddenly. "I have spent the night under your roof and shared your food. Is there something you need that I might get for you, in return for kindnesses?"

"You are leaving then?" asked Andara.

Could he smell leave-taking as he could smell fear? Ree wondered. Aloud he answered, "Yes, I have a message for Renka, the wife of the weaver."

Andara chuckled. "Ah, that message," he said. "Renka's had it many a time. She no longer believes it."

He pondered a little. "Perhaps she's right, Renka's sister. Perhaps she should not come. Lastra the weaver and Renka are rather dull uninteresting people. Their children are very like them. No one of them is half so entertaining as a cufflebird." He laughed again. "And then perhaps she's wrong, Renka's sister, Brada. Perhaps she should come to discover how wise she is to stay at home. And too it's time she learned that the bellbirds and the greening beetles can go on existing quite well without her to watch them."

"Still I must try to deliver the message, as I promised," said Ree, although indeed he could not think why. Only because it was a good excuse to be out and gone, to meet whatever lay ahead of him.

The blind man picked up his card and comb and began to work. "Then you can deliver another message. You can tell Lastra that I have yarn for him," he said briskly. "I am in need of flour and oil. Ask him not to bring too great a quantity, for they spoil in the heat. Only enough to last twenty days or so, if that is convenient."

His hands worked busily on. He seemed to want to say something more but did not know how to find the words. Finally he said slowly, "Do not fear Tarem. He is full of cunning, he is clever enough in his own way. He knows how to take advantage of people's weaknesses. But not their strengths."

Ree could not reply, it was a statement he did not wholly understand. He gathered up his blanket, still damp, and pulled it across his shoulders.

"I will take the message to Lastra if I can," he answered. "I am grateful for your help."

The blind man smiled. "I think I have been more hindrance than help to you," he said. "Or perhaps not. I would give you food except that I have none. Watch the trees for dove fruit, they are good and they grow all along the shores. And the big roundish beach roots are very satisfying. You will know them because the vines are covered with prickles. Even a blind man can recognize them with ease."

"Thank you," Ree answered. "I—I must go."

"Go then," said the blind man. His hands went on combing and combing. His face and his voice were tranquil. Ree wished he might stay.

He went quickly, through the door of the hut and out into the day. The air was like a blanket when it had been scrubbed with lather leaves, clean and damp and limp. The sun shone through thin mists, too vague to be clouds, and the jungle steamed. Along the river great flocks of birds flapped and fished and swum and dived.

Ree stood still. He had supposed Tarem would be waiting for him, to seize him as he stepped from the door, but there was no sign of the conjurer, or anybody else.

After a few moments he walked toward the river's edge, not supposing that he would be safer there but simply that he would be less apt to be taken by surprise. Along the banks brush was sparse, Tarem would have to come for his prize openly and without subterfuge. Ree would know when it was going to happen.

Not that he had a chance of escape. He could not run from the conjurers, they were too many, grown men, with dondaris. And he could not swim away in the river, for no doubt they were better swimmers than he. He was trapped. Soon they would have him in their barred box, to haul about and exhibit, to show to anyone who wished to stare at his disease.

He walked on. The river grew wider and slower. At

one place yesterday's storm had dug beneath the bank and the earth had slid down into the river. Through the clear water Ree watched small fishes swimming in and out among the coarse grasses and pink and yellow flowers. There was even a little frog clinging thoughtfully to a weed stalk.

What a strange world, thought Ree, and what curious things can happen in it. The fishes nosed at the pink blossoms. What a strange world, for here he was, as bewildered as the fishes in their new country, not knowing where to seek help or shelter, headed for imprisonment in that cage, and no more able to help himself than the grass which had slid down into the current —and no more responsible than the fishes for what had happened. All he could do was go on.

The little huts once again surprised him. He was walking among them before he realized they were there, so naturally they blended into the jungle's edge and the scrubby copses along the riverbank. Perhaps it was no longer the river but the lake. He thought it must be. Lastra's house must be close by.

At least he would be able to deliver his messages. He did not like to think he would not be able to repay kindnesses.

He could see people moving about among the dwellings, but he did not go up to any of them. He was afraid, somehow. Now that Tarem knew his secret he thought perhaps everyone would discover it.

Ah, well, they will all know soon enough, he told

himself at last and made his way to the nearest house.

Outside the door a man stooped over a heap of rugs and blankets and cloth, tying them into parcels with sinews. Ree came slowly toward him. The man was working very fast, making tight swift knots, pulling the cords hard, panting a little, muttering to himself. When Ree came close, he stopped and stared at him.

"Do you want to trade?" he asked.

Ree almost laughed. What would he trade? And why?

"No," he replied. "I am looking for the weaver, Lastra, and his wife Renka."

"I am Lastra," the man stated a trifle impatiently, turning back to his work. "Have you something to trade?"

"No," said Ree. "I have only a message for you from Andara. He has yarn to barter for flour and oil. Only a little flour and oil, enough for twenty days. And your wife's sister has sent word that she might come to visit you some day."

Lastra did not answer. Neither of these communications seemed of much importance to him. He went on tying his bundles. When he had done, he said pleadingly, "Would you help me carry these? They are heavy and I must hurry."

Carry them where? Ree asked himself. How far and how fast? But he did not speak, he simply picked up those bundles nearest him and shouldered them and waited. Lastra gathered up the others and set off, with Ree following.

"Thank you very much," gasped Lastra as they walked. "There is a market, my wife and children have gone on before me. I hope to trade many of my rugs and blankets. But I must be there very soon, before other weavers bring their goods."

Ree looked ahead. Along the forest edge some tents and canopies had been erected and people walked among them. He had not seen such a thing before, although he knew that when the True Men left the wide valley it was to such gatherings that they went, to get iron for knives or leather for various uses. Only in very hard times indeed did the True Men not supply all their own wants, except metals and some few other things.

He was suddenly pleased. He would like seeing such an assemblage and its wares.

Surely, in such a crowd, Tarem would not dare to seize him—if Tarem were there.

And surely among all these people there might be one who, like Ree, was frightened and alone. Perhaps someone who would recognize him as a boy stricken by chance and deprived of his own real self.

He could hope to meet such a someone. They would know each other on sight. And the knowledge would perhaps ease his heart's cold ache.

10

Lastra's wife and children waited under a tree, with some cloth already displayed over a small wooden frame. Lastra looked at it frowningly as he and Ree set down their burdens.

"This is not a good place," he said. "The light is not the best for showing the fineness of the weave. The color is dimmed too."

Renka and the two older children stared gravely at the material. Renka walked around it.

"Perhaps you are right," she agreed. "But when the sun begins to set, perhaps we should move it back here."

Lastra leaned over and touched the stuff with his hand. "Anyway, there is some cloth I would rather put out for showing now," he said. "The thread is a little finer and it has a sheen to it."

Renka answered, "But don't you think this design is best of all the designs?"

They all studied the cloth closely. Ree stood in silence. After a while Lastra opened a bundle and took out a second piece and held it up beside the first. A man came to inspect both pieces.

"I have oil," he said. "I am looking for a blanket."

Renka continued to stare at the two pieces of cloth, first one, then the other. Lastra took a blanket from one of the parcels and shook it out before the man.

"Vibon hair of the best quality," he said. "We are master weavers. You will not find a better blanket anywhere than this."

He touched it the way he had touched the cloth. The man said, "It is not heavy enough for my needs."

Lastra responded, "It is woven more tightly than most."

The man went away. Renka said, "You are right, I think. This second piece will look better." She carefully folded up the first piece and put it aside and flung the second over the small frame to exhibit it.

Ree came a little nearer. The cloth was very fine. Among the True Men no one could weave such stuff, smooth and subtly colored and close. Certainly Renka and Lastra and their children should be proud of such work.

But Ree soon grew weary of listening to them talk. They compared this piece and that, one blanket and the other, as though they themselves had never seen them before. They talked about the threads and the weaving, and argued about what perhaps might have made a better piece of fabric and what perhaps had not, as though anything could be done about it now.

A woman came and traded dried fish for the length of goods, and Lastra told her over and over about the skills that had gone into making it. When she left, he touched it one last time, Renka looked after it with regretful eyes. They began to discuss once again the choice of a cloth to drape over the frame.

It was plain to Ree that weaving was all they ever thought or spoke about. Brada did well to stay with her cufflebirds. Only the youngest of the three children ever looked away from the goods or seemed interested in what was going on around her. A girl a year or so younger than Merma, but short and plump, not bony and long-legged like Merma. She smiled at him and then turned her head, overcome by shyness.

Slowly Ree backed away from the others. He did not wish to interrupt their earnest discussion of blankets. There was nothing further for him to say. He had told them what he had been asked to tell them by Brada and Andara. Now he would leave. They went on talking about weaving vibon hair and reed fibers and did not notice his going.

If Tarem had appeared and tied him up with ropes, would they have come to his aid? Would they have even noticed it?

It seemed unlikely.

At first he did not know which way he should go. It was dusty and noisy and confusing here, people shouted and called, ponies neighed and dondaris made their mournful honks. Wherever the True Men went, there were always gentle sounds, music and laughter. This racket hurt his ears and disturbed him. Perhaps he had been wrong to come here or to hope for help from any of these loud and busy people.

He went on to watch a big man seated cross-legged and bargaining for the knives that lay before him on a rug, and for bits of iron that could be beaten and shaped into blades.

It was for such lumps that the True Men came to these gatherings, trading whatever goods they might have. Shaping a knife took a long hard time, yet Ree could see that none of the knives offered here would do for the tasks his people performed. The tools looked sharp and wicked, but not rugged and useful.

And anyway, the man would not surrender one of them for the simple wares that the True Men offered. Only one knife changed hands while Ree watched, and the man who got it gave in return a huge pile of the skins of some sort of animal, light in color, rich-looking in the sun. Beyond the knife-maker's tent, a woman peddled wooden buckets and barrels. Well made and strong, such things would be treasured by Ree's own people. Ree admired them, but he found them less interesting than the knives and blankets.

As he turned away, something touched his hand and he looked down. The weaver's tiny daughter stood beside him. She smiled at him again and he laid his palm on her shoulder in recognition. She must have followed him. Perhaps she too was bored with all the talk about warps and woofs. She should not be wandering alone, he thought. She might easily get lost. He would take her back to Renka and Lastra.

But not quite yet. People had gathered to watch something and Ree wished to see too. He took the child's hand.

"Shall we see what those people are looking at?" he asked. "Just for a moment. And then I'll take you back to your family."

"I can go back alone," she told him solemnly. He doubted it. She was so small, the world must be so far above her head. How could she find her way?

"I want to see too," she added. "Then I will go back, by myself."

Inside the circle of watchers a man was dancing. Barefoot, shirtless, dressed only in tight skin trousers, he leaped and twirled to a rhythm and a music he alone could hear. His chest and shoulders glistened with sweat, but that was the only sign of effort he showed. He seemed boneless, weightless. Ree had never before seen such a dancer, who could hover in the air like a bird. And he had a strange feeling that if everybody walked away, the dancer would go on dancing, for some secret reason of his own, as Brada's bellbirds would go on singing if she left them and came to visit Renka and her family.

The man danced and danced and only stopped when he could go on no longer. He slumped to the ground like a shot bird. Ree and the little girl stood hoping he would get up and dance again. But he lay still and, the crowd began to disperse.

At last Ree said, "He is not going to dance any more. We must go back to your mother and father." He led the child through the gathering. There were so many people—even at an important council meeting Ree had never seen such a lot of people. The two of them were thrust aside by a big man in a hurry and shoved by a woman carrying a jar of oil so large she could not see where she was going.

Ree lost his sense of direction and was not sure how to get back to Renka and Lastra and their piles of cloth. He saw a man holding a length of fabric in his hands and tried to reach him, to ask where he had got it. The man disappeared into the throng before Ree could call out to him.

Following the direction he thought the man had come from, they found a weaver, but it was not Lastra. The cloth this weaver had on display was coarser and harsher than even the True Men were accustomed to.

Still the colors were bright and bold and Ree thought it looked cheerful. He wished the weaver luck.

"Have you something to barter?" the weaver asked and Ree shook his head. He was going to ask if the man knew where Lastra and Renka might be found, when the little girl cried excitedly, "Look! Look! The conjurers! They have magic. Everything they bring with them is magic, my sister says."

She pulled at his arm to make him come with her. Ree saw them straight ahead: Tarem and all his family. There was the woman who had fed the fire, the boy who had been with him in the earthquake, even the baby still crying drearily.

"It is not magic," Ree said sharply. "It is foolishness. No one believes it is magic."

The little girl answered in a sulky voice, "It is magic. All my family knows it is magic. My mother and my father know."

Not Renka and Lastra, Ree told himself. They would not believe in magic, only in weaving. He himself thought that weaving must be a kind of magic. He remembered the wads of vibon hair he used to find in the wide valley. He remembered Andara's hands pulling and patting the dull stuff. A kind of magic that it should end as the soft and smooth and beautifully colored cloths that Renka and Lastra had brought to the market.

The child drew away from him and began to squeeze in among the people. She was determined to reach the conjurers' encampment. And it was an encampment. The goods they had brought were spread out on a low table, but Tarem and his family, the dondaris, and even the wheeled box with its hateful bars, were ranged around a hearthfire as though they intended to stay for months.

Or for that matter as though they might leave in an hour.

Tarem had not yet seen him, Ree was certain. He could disappear into the mob and he and the conjurer need never meet again.

Yet Ree was uneasy about the weaver's child. He should have taken her back to Renka at once, not wandered about until the day had begun to ebb and the swarm of men and women had grown so huge.

Reluctantly he followed her. "Come along," he called. "We must go back."

"I want to see," she answered over her shoulder. Ree stopped. He would go no closer.

It was too late. The sand-colored eyes of Tarem and his son and the others gazed at him steadily.

Ree stared back. He would not be afraid. He was sure they would do nothing to him here. Almost sure. Not as sure as he had been when he first reached the market. Perhaps all these people believed in Tarem's magic powers. Perhaps they were all afraid of him. At any rate Ree would not let the conjurers think he was afraid.

He pushed on through the crowd and found the

little girl and reached for her hand, but a man thrust himself between them.

"Will you take this leather thong for its weight in the powder to keep away snakes?" he asked anxiously. Tarem's wife took the thong and looked it over and then carefully weighed out a little powder from a gourd bowl.

"This much," she said, and poured it into the man's hand and he looked at it doubtfully, but then went away.

Ree was again standing next to the weaver's child.

"These things do not look like magic," she said fretfully. She was growing tired, he thought, and probably hungry. And indeed the stained leather sacks and bowls on the table were dull to look at. Nothing seemed strange or mysterious, in spite of Tarem's wife's whispers about charms and granted wishes and long life.

She had overheard the little girl's complaint and said at once, "It is all true magic." Her voice was like the sound of sand trickling steadily down upon rock, monotonous, gentle. "This potion will make you well loved, and these crystals are talismans to bring luck. Real magic. And this—" she pointed to a pile of pods—"this is the greatest and truest magic of all."

The child extended her hand as if to pick up one of the seed cases.

Tarem's wife caught her wrist and exclaimed, "No! You—"

"It is all foolishness!" cried Ree. "That is nothing but a seed pod!"

He snatched it up to look at it carefully. Tarem's wife gasped.

"It is only the pod of a gadran tree. I have seen—" he broke off. The spines on the pod had pricked his fingers deeply. "I have seen them before. A few of the trees grow on the High Plains."

He bit his lip. He had not meant to mention the High Plains. His fingers stung and burned. His hand burned. It was growing dark and darker, and the sky was settling down close to earth and shadows fell over and around him and pushed him steadily to the ground . . .

11

REE WOKE not as from sleep but as from death, from some bottomless dreamless lightless pit of unconsciousness. He heard voices, Tarem's voice and the soft voice of Tarem's wife. He was aware that these were voices he recognized, that he knew the speakers, but he could not remember their names or their faces.

He dreamed, and the dreams too were full of faceless people, who spoke in gentle tones and held him firmly so that he could not move. He did not struggle, there seemed nothing to struggle against, the hands that grasped him he could scarcely feel. He only knew they were there and he drifted in and out of darkness for days and weeks—and then he was awake.

There were no hands, there were no voices, he was alone. He lay with his eyes shut, for he believed he must be in that cage. He believed that the first thing he would see would be those hateful bars.

The air was close and hot and still. His head ached and he was hungry and thirsty, terribly thirsty. At last he opened his eyes and saw that he was not in the cage, he was in Tarem's cart.

The conjurers had made sure he would not get out and that no one would get in to see their marvelous captive. A skin had been draped over the single window and the window was shuttered and bolted from outside. Ree stumbled to the door and tried it cautiously and it too was locked.

He did not know whether it was day or night, how long a time he had lain in his trance, or if the conjurers had moved him from the market. He moved unsteadily around the walls. The wagon was not carefully or truly built, but it was stout enough. To escape from it would not be easy.

By and by he discovered a crack in the side, light fell faintly through it. He went to the crack and put his face against it, glad of the fresh air. When he felt better, he looked out.

The world was in a kind of twilight, either late evening or early morning. He could see nothing except, dimly, the jungle's edge. But after a few moments the light grew stronger.

So it was a new day. Sounds came from somewhere on the other side of the cart and he thought they must still be at the market.

What will they do with me? Ree thought. Will they put me in the cage? Will people give them oil and skins and dried meat to see me and touch me? Or will they kill me and sell me in bits as they would have done the two-headed goat?

The baby began its dreary wailing. Someone passed by the caravan, too close for Ree to make out more than a quick blur. Farther away he could see people moving about.

All at once he drew in his breath sharply. Coming out of the edge of the jungle there, those two men, he knew them! They were two of the True Men, Dreen and Harna, he was almost certain. They were coming straight toward the caravan.

When they came closer, he would call out to them.

They would make Tarem release him. Even though Kadir had said Ree was no longer one of the True Men, they would not leave anyone to such a fate. They were brave men and quick to aid those in trouble, like all the True Men. They would not leave him to be stared at and poked at in a barred box.

They were almost near enough. He wished his throat were not so dry. He watched them come. Harna said something and Dreen laughed and looked up and then in turn spoke to Harna. They did not pause, they simply turned aside and walked away out of Ree's sight.

He sank to his knees. He should have known they would not come near the sorcerers. The True Men avoided such people. They would have nothing to do with those who pretended to have magic or with those foolish enough to believe in those pretensions.

And what could they do for him anyway? They might force Tarem to let him out of the caravan, but the conjurer would think of a way to get him back. Even Andara had said Tarem was clever.

Perhaps there was nothing left in the world for him but to be caged like a wild thing and stared at by anyone. How easily he had fallen into Tarem's hands! He should have expected something like the little jabs on his fingers that had let the drug into his body. He knew about such things. He had been stupid and deserved his fate.

He could not escape. Tarem would put him in that box. If he protested, Tarem would prick him with the drug and he would lie sleeping while people stared at him, while they touched him. One day he would die in his sleep and Tarem would cut off his ears and fingers and call them magic tokens and trade them for salt and furs.

He groaned softly. He could not think why this had happened to him. Surely it hadn't happened. It was a thing he had dreamed or a sickness in his brain, he would look up and all would be well again, and he would be out with his pony—

He raised his face from his hands and saw Tarem's

dim scruffy caravan with its rough furnishings and along the walls the strings of drying herbs and the bottles and bags. He thought suddenly how dreadful it would be to discover that they were indeed magicians and healers; if they did indeed possess the power to heal him. For they would never be willing to do so. What use would he be to them once his disease had gone away?

How could he be so foolish? All these things along the walls were simply ordinary things, like the gadran pod, collected because they had a curious look or a strong scent, making them seem impressive to anyone to whom they were unfamiliar.

Even the poison that had made him drop to sleep was no enchantment and no medicine. It was the juice of a plant and it could do this simple thing only, make one fall deeply asleep.

There was no magic. There was no cure for him. By chance a thing had happened and he would not know why, any more than he would know why the journey stick pointed one way rather than another when Kadir threw it in the air.

The door opened, and Tarem and his wife came in, followed by the boy and another of the men. They came in swiftly, crowded together, and hastily slammed the door behind. Ree did not even trouble to rise from the floor. Tarem's eyes lit up.

"Ah, you are awake," he said. He came to him and offered a wooden bowl full of some liquid. Ree hesitated. It might be some potion to put him again into a state of sleep or at least of listlessness.

He took the bowl and drank.

The drink was cool and tart and he swallowed it all. The second man and woman and the boy stared at him. Tarem turned to them.

"Do you see?" he asked triumphantly. "Is it not a wonder surpassing all other wonders? Oh, did I not tell you?"

Tarem's wife slowly drew close to Ree. She knelt beside him and brought her face close to his. She moved her hand along his arm, not touching, holding it an inch or so above his skin as though she expected to feel some warmth or even cold, some sensation different from the one provided by ordinary flesh. Then she did press her hand lightly to his hand for a tiny space.

"What is it?" she asked in her whispery voice. "What makes it? Is it real magic? I have never seen anything so strange! It must be real magic."

"What is magic?" asked Tarem roughly.

The woman stood up and then Ree stood too. She was still looking at him with awe. The second man put a finger to Ree's shoulder, as though to make sure the boy was really there or, like the woman, to determine if the glow gave forth heat or some other feeling.

"My name is Nalla," he began. "Where do you come from? Are there others like you?"

"He's one of the True Men," Tarem interruped. "Anyone can see that."

"I am no one and come from nowhere and there is no one else like me," Ree answered sullenly.

Tarem shrugged. "No matter," he said. "Whoever he is, we are lucky to have found him. This will bring us wealth we have not dreamed of before, another dondari and ponies and a better cart. We will be powerful and we will possess much. The best of knives and the finest of blankets. We will eat honey with every meal."

"We will need a tent," put in Nalla. "Made of skins of the most excellent qualities, so they can be stitched together very carefully. Even at noon no light will penetrate."

"And it must be large," Tarem added. "So that several people can be admitted at one time. Once they are inside and see him, then they will be allowed to touch. But they must give something beyond what they have given to be allowed to see him, if they wish to touch."

"Yes, a good deal more," said Nalla, consideringly. "It is one thing to see a wonder, but another to touch it and make sure it is a true wonder. And we can tell them to touch him guarantees luck and long life."

Ree thought of those stroking prodding hands. He thought of the staring eyes and the faces full of curiosity, regarding him as they would a gadran pod, without kindness or fellow feeling or even pity.

Did Tarem and Nalla not know or care what they were doing? When they looked at him, it was obvious that they did not really see a boy or even his shining skin. What they were seeing was jars of oil and sacks of flour. What they were seeing was ponies.

His glance swept over all of them. Tarem's wife still regarded him with awe. But Tarem's son! What Ree saw in the sand-colored boy's eyes startled him beyond measure. That other boy was dazzled, excited—and envious!

Tarem's son was envious. He wished this hideous thing had happened to him! With all his heart he longed to be the one who sat in the tent to be gaped at and fingered like a new blanket.

The other boy's dullness made Ree strangely angry and gave him sudden courage. He turned his head and gazed at Tarem and Nalla.

"How could you be so certain this is not magic?" he asked loudly. "Because your silly soups and rocks are not magic, why do you suppose magic cannot be?"

Inside the caravan his voice sounded in his own ears thin and shaky. But to the others it must have seemed different.

"Hush," warned Tarem. "Those outside might hear."

"This might be magic, in truth," Ree went on, "and magic of the most evil sort. I might have it in myself to give you not long life and good luck, but illness and misery and sorrow."

"I knew it was magic," Tarem's wife whispered.

"We meant to share all things with you," Nalla said

hurriedly. "You shall have a swift pony of your own and furs to wear. We will share fairly."

"It may be that those who touch my skin turn leprous and diseased," Ree went on. "It may be that those who put their hands on my hands will be consumed by fire in the bones, will die a dreadful death."

Tarem's wife moaned. Tarem almost whined. "We promise to share fairly. You shall have anything you want, and more. Alone you could not manage to make such a tent or to lure people in to see."

"You do not believe I am a demon then?" Ree's voice sounded louder.

"I have never seen a demon," said Tarem cautiously. "I have not seen any magic thing."

"But you have never seen anything like me before?" pressed Ree.

"No, no," cried the conjurer. "I have already said so. It was luck that I saw you at Andara's, and greater luck that you handled the gadran pod. You—"

He broke off. A little shadow of fear narrowed his eyes.

"It—it is not so, is it?" he asked. "You are not speaking the truth?"

"No," answered Ree wearily. "It is not so. I am not a demon. Only Ree, to whom a thing has happened. Only Ree, and not a goat with two heads. I am human. I will not live in your tent or your barred box. Not even for the finest honey and the softest furs."

He reached forward quickly and raised the latch on the door. "Wait!" cried Tarem. "Stop!"

It was too late. Ree stood framed in the dark doorway. And the cloudy night lay all around him and the glow from his bones made a beacon of him in the shadows.

Someone cried aloud, in astonishment and fear. For the space of a second Ree thought it must have been his own voice ringing out in the dimness. He took a backward step, but it was too late. Tarem's hand shoved him sharply forward.

There were more shouts, and people came running. Even those who had left the market and were making their way toward their homes turned back to see what was taking place. A murmuring clamor swept through the tents and stalls.

Ree stood on the little ladder leading up into the cart and watched the crowd that gathered in the faint light of the few lanterns and torches scattered here and there. He had no one but himself to blame for this betrayal. The "dawn" he had observed when he

peered through the crack in Tarem's wagon, the beginning of a new day, had been no such thing. It had
been only a cloud passing away from the setting sun
or a sudden twilight flare of scarlet, such as often
happened when the sky was overcast.

He had slept no more than an hour or so under the
influence of Tarem's drug on the spiny gadran pod.
He had been still heavy-headed and muddled during
his talk with the conjurers, he had not given himself
time to think clearly, to consider what was wise to do.
He had simply walked out into the night, out into the
middle of the market, for everyone to see.

"Look! Look!" "Who is it?" "What is it?" The voices
came from here and there, excited, wondering.

Ree could imagine how they saw him, standing there
in the black doorway. He had no blanket; he had lost
it somewhere in his long dreams. He saw himself as
they must see him, with light coming softly through
the worn coarse fabric of his shirt; with his arms and
hands and face and throat covered with nothing at all
except the pale fire of his own existence.

Suddenly the wailing baby shrieked as if in an agony
of fright and then a man shouted harshly, "A monster!
A monster! The sorcerers have created a monster!"

Behind Ree Tarem answered, as roughly and strongly
as so sleek a voice might manage.

"He's naught to do with us. He handled one of those
charms we have ever warned must not be touched. Its

magic put him to sleep and we gave him an antidote,
out of kindness. He was diseased before he came here.
I know, for I saw him at Andara's, nights ago. We want
no dealings with him nor he with us. If this is magic,
it is not our kind of magic."

In spite of his fear Ree felt a flash of scorn for
Tarem. Only a few minutes ago he had been willing
enough to deal with the "monster."

The knife-trader called out mockingly, "Can you not
cure him then, conjurer?"

And Tarem's answer was swift: "Your wares would
make the best cure."

Terror settled over Ree like an icy rain, and he
trembled. Would one of those narrow lovely deadly
blades come gliding through the air, to enter his eye
or his heart and put an end to all his troubles? He
trembled and waited, but the knife-vendor made no
move.

The circle of watchers stood and stared. Ree could
wait no longer. He would step down from the cart and
walk away.

Would they stone him, tear him to bits, cast him into
a great fire? Then they must do so. He would not stand
there longer, waiting and trembling.

He took a step to the ground and those nearest him
drew back, gasping and exclaiming.

Let me leave, he wished to say. I cannot harm you,
I do not wish to harm you. I am Ree, one of the True

Men, a human boy to whom a thing has happened. Let me go.

But he had no voice, his throat was closed with dread. For who could believe such a thing? Who could look at this unnatural radiant creature and suppose it could be one of the True Men? Even Ree, seeing himself through their eyes, found it hard to believe. How could he still be Ree, the arrow-swift, the arrow-straight, when this thing had happened to him and made him something else?

Up till this moment it had not occurred to him that anything more than a great misfortune had befallen him, as misfortunes befall all men sooner or later. Now suddenly it had become a real and terrifying possibility that Ree no longer existed, had been changed into something hateful and inhuman.

Was it true? Was he so changed that never again would men and women think of him as one of them?

It could not be true. It could not be. They must know it was not true.

He made himself take a pace and a pace slowly toward the throng, and they parted before him. They made way for him and yet there was an ominous feeling as of a threatening storm, and it came not from the winds and sky but from the circle of perplexed and frightened watchers.

They would kill him, Ree thought desolately. They would kill him because they would not know what else to do with him, as he himself did not know how to find a place in the world or how to become accustomed to his own strangeness and exile.

He went on, taking cautious steady steps, and his eyes moved over the crowd. Was there not someone there to think of him as a fellow being, a body of flesh and blood, not some grotesque blunder of the universe or some ill-omened bit of sorcery?

He saw the knife-vendor with a face as hard and sharp as his wares. He saw Tarem's son, slipping in and out among the crowd, with a mouth still greedy for excitement and sensation. He saw Lastra and Renka standing some way ahead.

Did they not remember him? Did they not recall that a boy, like any other boy, had helped them carry the bundles to market? Had brought Renka a message of love and regret from her sister?

They did not meet his gaze. They would not look into his eyes. They would not acknowledge the presence of a child like one of their own children.

The crowd fell away before him. He could feel it fall in behind. Between his shoulder blades he felt their hostile stares as any minute he would feel, he knew, the thump of stone or the sharp slash of knife-blade. Yet he did not turn and did not stop. Fear made his body almost rigid and made his feet move without his will, and he could not stop.

Around him the menacing whispers rose and fell

like the sound of a wind among the trees, and he walked on. And suddenly his way was barred.

Renka stood in his path. No, she was coming toward him, and he hesitated and then at last stood still.

She frightened him more than ever. Her face was calm and smooth, she did not look into his eyes, she came toward him purposefully and intently. She meant to be the first to strike him, to lead the way for others to take up sticks and stones and beat him to death. He watched her come, and when she raised her hand, he tried not to flinch. He stood frozen and waiting and all about him the whispers ceased and the silence grew and waited too. Softly she touched the sleeve of his shirt. Her voice on the still night air was clear and sweet and plainly heard.

"How beautiful!" she marveled. "Oh, how very beautiful! If only I might find a thread with such a sheen, to weave a shirt that looked like that!"

For a moment Ree could not make out her words. He was too stunned to take in what she had said. It was so different from what he had believed she would say, believed she would do.

And then he burst out laughing. He could not help himself. He had expected hate and fury, if not death. The whole crowd had expected it and possibly hoped for it and wished for Renka to make the first move.

And then what she had done turned out to be something so different; relief and surprise combined to make him laugh and the sound of his own laughter made him laugh still more. He had not laughed in many days and now he found it hard to stop.

Someone near him began to laugh, a little nervously, and someone else, and then all of them, laughing more and more until they were all laughing, nearly weeping with laughter.

Ree had forgot that laughter could also make one weep.

But at last the laughter slowed and stopped and once more there was silence. The menace was gone, or nearly gone. Once again Ree tried to speak: I am a human boy. I have no desire to trouble or unsettle anyone. I cannot harm you and do not wish to harm you. I will go and disturb you no longer.

The words were there, they hung in the air, he could almost hear them, but he could not say them. He walked forward again, leaving Renka with her hand outstretched and all the others with their staring faces. He walked neither fast nor slow and held his head straight and let them look. Long after he had left the market he knew their eyes were watching and watching. He knew what an eerie and astounding figure he must be to them. They would be able to see him for a great distance in the starless gloom.

He reached the edge of the lake and made his way along its shore. The sand underfoot was smooth and hard-packed and he did not stumble or find it necessary to turn from his course. Not that he knew what his course was, only to travel on and on while his legs could carry him.

Once again he thought how foolish he had been. Why had he supposed that daylight and a blanket would conceal him forever and ever? Sooner or later the world was bound to see him as he really was, without disguise, with no cave in which to shelter. Sooner or later the world was bound to know that this wanderer was that one of the True Men who had been rejected. Sooner or later everyone would know what was real and the truth. He walked.

The water rippled softly against the sandy beach. From the jungle a night bird screamed frantically and nearby there was the purring voice of an insect, like nothing he had ever heard before. Here even the voices of night were different from anything he had ever known, not simply unfamiliar but of a new kind and quality compared to all the loved aspects of life as it had been before. Where his heart had been there was a feeling of nothingness and numbness.

The moon glimmered faintly through the clouds, and seeing it, he wished he might be transported to the moon—the moon, which gleamed through the ragged clouds as his skin gleamed through his worn shirt, and whose light was only seen at night. He must belong not on the earth but on the moon. Surely he would be welcomed there if he could find the way.

He walked and walked. And behind him terror and despair crept like great stalking cats.

13

WHEN he woke, the day was already half gone. The sun shone and only a terrible weariness of body and of spirit had kept him sleeping beneath its brightness.

He staggered to his feet and stared out across the lake where it stretched away to the world's edge. There must be no farther shore, the lake must simply go on and on until it poured out into space, at the end of the earth. Over its surface an eagle flew with long, even, up-and-down strokes of its great wings and then suddenly dove, falling, falling, splashing into the water with wide grasping talons. The fish escaped, the eagle rose swiftly into the air and shrieked angrily.

Hungry. The eagle was hungry. Ree was hungry too,

famished. It had been a long time since he had shared the bread and dove fruit with Andara. He searched for food and came on some bushes covered with plump pods. He ate the peas, pods and all, and they were faintly sweet and filling and good. He gathered all he could find and set out walking again.

He followed the lake's edge and now the jungle came closer and closer. It made him uneasy. He did not like having that palisade of trees and vines, hiding all its dangers, so near. He did not like the thought that he might have to enter it again. He looked about and could see no one and no sign of human habitation, only the heavy fence of greenery that kept the jungle in—or the world of air and sunlight out.

Still he went on, walking at a steady pace along the sandy shore. Beside him his shadow grew longer and longer and the mist of dusk crept over the water. The air was warm and still, and as it grew darker, he could glance down and see the first faint glow along his wrists and fingers. He did not look down again but walked on and on, and tried to keep his thoughts on the even rhythm of his legs taking one step after another.

In spite of himself he thought again, and suddenly, of the wide valley and the evening fires and the ponies —the ponies! There was a pony coming toward him, one of the True Men's ponies, careening madly straight toward him over the flat beach!

He did not hesitate but ran and cast himself at it and

seized it by the mane and hung on. He was tired, more than a little shaky from lack of food. The pony reared and kicked and almost broke his grip, but he had dealt with ponies many times. He threw all his weight against it and circled its neck with his arm and clung on until the terrified animal slowed and finally halted with heaving lathered sides.

Ree stood by it quietly, holding it firmly, speaking softly. Perhaps it would be once more frightened by the sight of him, he thought, and tried to keep out of range of the eyes in the drooping head. He patted it gently, and when in a bit it seemed calmer, he guided it slowly down to the water's edge and it drank a little, and when it turned its head and saw him, it did not shy away. He was grateful.

This must be the pony he had seen with Dreen and Harna. What had happened? What had frightened the little animal so? Where were Dreen and Harna? He considered walking in the direction from which the pony had come, but it was still trembling and obviously exhausted. Together they waited by the lake, and the moon rose in a clear sky, so that Ree was relieved. He was a less conspicuous figure in the moon's merciful glow which half-drowned his own.

Nonetheless the man walking toward him recognized him long before they met.

"Young Ree!" he called and quickened his steps. "Young Ree! You've got the pony. I thought we'd lost it forever!"

Ree was silent for a moment, thinking only to let Dreen take the pony away, but curiosity made him speak.

"What happened? What frightened the pony?" he burst out. "Where is Harna and why are you here?"

Dreen did not seem to resent being questioned. "We came to the market to barter for knives. We are in need," he explained. "But the man with whom we like to trade was not there. So we went on, to the house where he lives. We traveled late last night and made our bargain this morning and set out for the wide valley almost at once. We should have rested longer, the pony was tired and so were we. We kept on, and then when we made our camp, we chose the wrong place, too close to the jungle. Before we could build our fire or hobble the pony, a big spotted ganio leaped for us and the pony bolted. Harna and I chased it and Harna tripped in the dark and hurt his leg. He could not keep up, and I have left him there."

His voice grew troubled. "Now I must go and fetch him, and I am worried about the pony. I do not wish to tire it further, but if I hobble it and leave it here, the ganio may kill it. It has our scent, I'm sure."

"Go fetch Harna," said Ree. "I will stay with the pony. No ganio or any other cat will come close to us," he added evenly.

Dreen stared at him a moment and then muttered, "Perhaps you are right." He looked away in embarrassment and then went on.

"I would be grateful. It was a stupid thing we did and we are fortunate that you were here."

Ree stroked the pony's rough haunch. Such things come about by chance, he wanted to say. Chance rules the True Men. But he did not speak.

Dreen hobbled the pony and disappeared into the night. Ree stood by the little animal and scratched its head and spoke to it now and then. It nuzzled at his shirt and he remembered the few peas he had put there, to eat later. He took them out and fed them to the pony and it ate from his shining hand as though it were used to such things.

When the ganio screamed once from the jungle's edge, the little horse did not seem too alarmed, only moved a little closer to him.

Later when Dreen came back with Harna limping beside him, they built a small fire and sat around it while Harna heated some oil to rub on his bruised leg and Dreen shared out a supper of bread and boiled roots. Except for the lake lying quiet under the quiet moon, Ree might have been home again in the wide valley. He might have been sitting with any of the True Men after a day of searching for peats and vibon hair. Here near the fire he might still be as he had once been, one of them and not a monster . . .

He looked up. He had not seen such a clear sky in many days. The stars were bright.

"The comet," he said. "Did the comet come?"

Harna answered, "We think not. The sky has been overcast and there has been much dust and haze from the earthquakes. We did not see the comet again, not even on the few nights when the clouds parted. It has been a bad time for Kadir. Perhaps it was not our comet at all. At any rate, we had to act as if it were not."

He sighed and lay down. Dreen too slept, and then Ree. Once he woke and heard Harna moving about, tending his bruised leg. Did he stare at the boy in the darkness? Ree did not open his eyes to see.

In the morning Dreen offered Ree some of the bread. "To take with you on your journey," he said. It was a dismissal. Dreen meant that Ree should go his own way as he had been doing when the pony came down the beach. In memory Ree saw once again Dreen and Harna turning aside from Tarem's cart.

Now he refused the bread. "You may need it worse than I," he pointed out. "The others are waiting for you, you should not have to stop to search for food."

Ree on the other hand had all the time in the world and must learn to accept the fact that no one waited for him or his help.

"Very well," said Harna. They, too, knew that the others waited. "Yet we wish you to know that we are grateful."

And then the two men turned away.

None of them said farewell. There was no farewell to be said. Ree watched till they were almost out of sight. He could see them for a long time, the two men and the little plodding pony. Two of the True Men and a pony, creatures out of place and strange away from the High Plains and the wide valley.

He turned and set out in the opposite direction, a boy out of place and strange in any corner of the earth. He saw a prickle-covered vine and remembered Andara's words about beach roots and stopped to dig this one up.

With his knife he cut it into pieces and ate it slowly. When he had done, he knelt to rinse his fingers and his knife in the lake. The sun was burning through the clouds and the water was a mirror, but he could not see himself reflected there.

It was true then? There was no Ree, no arrow-boy, born on the High Plains? He had been erased as the waves were wiping out the tracks of some small beast which had earlier walked along the water's edge.

He shifted to one side and saw himself plainly for a moment. Yet his face seemed unfamiliar, he scarcely recognized himself.

He rose and walked toward the jungle's edge, looking for a dove fruit tree. These things he knew were good to eat and he was still hungry—and would be hungrier yet as the day went on.

He found a tree full of fruits and reached up to pick one and a tiny tiny bird flickered away from beneath his fingers. Juice dripped from the scars its long bill had made in the skin of the fruit. Among the branches insects of every sort and color flew about, buzzing and ticking.

Ree stood holding the wounded dove fruit in his fingers. A lovely and fantastic world, but not his own. No wonder he was disappearing.

Something must happen. Perhaps he must change and be someone else. But he did not know how to change or whom to be in this strident gaudy land.

He began to gather those fruits which were least marred and pecked by the insects and birds, to carry with him as he went, wherever he might be going. There were few of them worth picking. He walked a little farther inside the green shadows, hoping to find another tree. He did not like being in that close dim world, with its eerie sounds and its feel of hostile presences back among the ferns. Yet he needed food.

While he was looking, he heard suddenly the sweet lilting voice of a bellbird. Brada's bellbird, whose song all summer long blended with the sound of wind and the ponies' bells over the High Plains. Even now the True Men would be gathering at the foot of the trail which led up to the Plains, even now the frost there would be melting from the meadows and the grass turning slowly green. Ree pressed into the jungle a little farther and by and by saw the bird, the little familiar brown bird, with beak pointed upward. The song swung up into the air and then fell away into a rippling trill and stopped. The bellbird gave a soft murmur of content and flew off.

How strange that so tiny a bird should make such a journey: to fly such distances twice a year, all its small life, following some unerring map in its head. The world was strange, all its shapes and colors, its changing seasons, its rivers and fields, and over it the ever-moving stars.

Ree stood a moment trying to follow the bird's flight, and then he twisted around a great tree and past some ferns. He had done with walking without purpose and heading for no place at all. He knew where he would go, at last.

THE JOURNEY through the jungle took all that day and the night and most of the second day. He found nothing to eat except occasional dove fruits, and under those trees were the marks of beasts which had come to share the feast, so that he was afraid to linger or to climb among the branches. He ate only the bruised and rotting fruits which lay on the ground.

He slept little and fitfully, without his blanket easy prey for insects of every kind. The snarls and screams of wild creatures woke him every few moments, and then he rose and walked again, as fearful of walking as of sleeping.

His feet swelled, his head swam. He made his way through wet boggy places, thinking at each step of quicksand which would swallow him slowly, like a snake swallowing its victim. He thought of snakes, coiled near his feet, stretched along limbs of trees, lying behind roots. He thought of being lost forever beneath that leafy haze, among the huge trunks. He could comfort himself only that he was never in the dark—and that was cold comfort. Surely sooner or later he would meet some predator who would not be over-awed by that light; who would find that moving glow irresistible. He could not hurry, and when he tried to force himself to move more swiftly, he was assailed with the dreadful notion that he might be hurrying in the wrong direction. When he stumbled at last out into the open air, for a moment he thought delirium had seized him. He could not believe he was truly outside.

He did not know where he was and he was hungrier than ever, but at least he could move more than a step at a time, at least he knew that the brush ahead of him did not shelter some great-toothed cat. He knew too that the mountains looming before him were those which rimmed the wide valley. If he should climb them and look straight across, he would see the High Plains. His eyes filled with tears. Once again he would see the High Plains.

He found a spring and some half-ripened berries and drank and ate and then slept, a long time. When he woke, he set out toward the mountains.

He came upon a road almost at once. It was steep and rough and untended, not one of the roads where the people of the Stone Towns worked and asked a toll at some narrow passage. That was fortunate, for certainly Ree had nothing to give as toll. But a little worrisome, for the road was hard to travel, and it must be too that he would come down into the wide valley in some spot likely not well known to him.

Still he climbed, stopping only to find food where he could and to drink at any spring or stream he came to. He was tired and what he had to eat was seldom satisfying, and by nightfall he knew he had come to the last trickle of water he would encounter for a long while. He slept near it. He would have a final drink in the morning.

The path wandered here and there, so that it was less steep than it had been. He was impatient to reach the crest of the mountains and hated all the bends and twists. Yet he knew he must follow the road. The way straight up the mountain was rough and he could see sheer cliffs at the very top.

It was afternoon before he arrived at the peaks. He was panting and hungry and thirsty again, but that moment was sweet and triumphant. He had done it.

He turned and looked down the craggy yellow slopes, down to the dark ribbon of the jungle, full of death and flowers, and past that to the vague blue mist of the lake. From this vantage he could see the far side, a deeper strip of mist along the world's edge. He was glad that something held the lake in and it did not fall gurgling out into space.

He stood for a long time, remembering the ugly Stone Towns and Brada's lovingly tended garden. Remembering the man at the fair, dancing his strange lone dance, and Andara's quiet voice and Tarem and the bellbird. Remembering all that had befallen him. And then he turned the other way.

Under a little canopy of cloud glistened the High Plains.

He had been right that he would descend the mountains into unfamiliar territory. It took some time for him to get his bearings, and even when he began to recognize landmarks he could scarcely believe it and had to go back twice to be sure the little bog was the one where he had gathered peats that last day, when he had still been one of the True Men.

He touched the rough grasses with his hands and stared around at the landscape in its soft dim colors. The wide valley! He was here once more!

The next morning he saw, far away, the smoke from hearthfires and by noon he could stand on a small hilltop and make out the carts clustered together at the foot of the trail which led to the High Plains.

That night he lay down to sleep close enough to hear the ponies stamping and snorting in the dark. His family was asleep there, and Kadir, and the other council members. And in the morning . . .

He woke early. He watched as a young woman approached him with her pony, setting out for a day's gleaning.

"Istra," he called softly, and she turned and came slowly to him. Her eyes were full of curiosity, but she asked no questions.

"You have grown very thin," she said.

"Would you go to the carts and ask Kadir if he would meet me here?" Ree requested.

After a moment she nodded and left the pony to graze and turned back.

Ree waited.

The head of the council walked toward him and Ree went to meet him. When they were almost face to face, Kadir spoke.

"Harna and Dreen have told us of your help. We are all grateful."

"It was a small thing," Ree said. He shrugged. "Ill luck befell them and I helped as I could. And I am glad to know they are safely back."

There was a long silence. Ree looked down at Kadir's arm, at a curious scar which he had acquired many years ago, so long ago that Ree scarcely saw the blemish, though it was wide and deep. A part of Kadir now.

At last Ree spoke. "The comet did not come?" he asked. "Dreen and Harna said—"

"The comet did not come," interrupted Kadir and his voice was mournful. "In the clear skies of the last two nights there was no sign. If it had been our comet, there would have been some sign of it surely. Stories say it lit the sky for many weeks."

Ree drew a deep breath. "Perhaps the comet will never be seen again," he ventured.

Kadir answered somberly, "The comet must come. It is the sign that the pact between us and earth will always be kept and that the High Plains will always be ours. We are the True Men."

Ree touched the leaves of a lather bush growing near him.

"The comet did not come and it may never come," he responded slowly. "Yet the True Men are the True Men still. The High Plains still belong to them and they still love the earth with all their hearts. Does not that love make them the True Men more than any pact, more than any sign?"

Kadir frowned. "What are you saying?" he asked.

Ree waited a while before he spoke. "I have come home," he said simply.

Kadir looked up the long blue slope of the mountain. "The council has decided that you must leave us," he said uneasily. Ree said nothing.

"A strange thing has happened to you," the head of the council went on. "And now you have gone a long way from us and become perhaps stranger still."

"The world is a strange place," Ree agreed. "The earth moves through the seasons, birds sing, and a comet appears in the sky. Wondrous things. And all men are strange, different one from another, some more so than others. Yet they are still men, are born and live a little while and die. I am come home."

Kadir's eyes were kind but gravely troubled.

"The council has decided—" he began, and Ree broke in fiercely, "Then you must kill me!"

Shock made Kadir's lips go gray. "Kill you!" he whispered. "We could not do such a thing."

Ree grasped the man's hard-muscled arm. "Listen," he cried, and struggled to make his words take the shape of all that he had seen and what his heart felt. "I am Ree, one of the True Men, born on the High Plains. A strange thing has befallen me as it might befall anyone, for strange and terrible things happen by chance, as rain falls by chance. It may be that what has happened to me is so strange and terrible that I may never again be one of the True Men. But if that is so, you must kill me. For away from the wide valley and the ponies and the High Plains, I cannot be Ree. I am not human, a wonder, a talisman, a shining thread."

He paused. Did Kadir understand? Could he not see somewhere in the depths of Kadir's eyes a little stir, a little fire of recognition?

"P-perhaps another boy, another person," he stammered, "might have discovered how to be the one to whom this happened and still not change, still be himself. Or might find a way to transform into some other being and live in another way. But that is not how it is with me. I am Ree and you must kill me, for I will not be what I am not and cannot be."

For a long while Kadir stood gazing into Ree's eyes, and though Ree said no more, with his eyes he hoped to tell the council head of Tarem's son and Renka's stroking hand and Padran's last sad laughter.

Kadir gently loosened Ree's grip on his arm and stood chafing the scar above his wrist. Nearby in a little blossoming tree the bellbird sang its sweet and joyous song.

"I will go now," Kadir said finally. "I will call the council together and tell them what you have said. We will discuss it."

He turned back toward the carts.

Over and over in his palm Ree rubbed with his thumb the pebbles and shells he had brought as a "present" for Merma.

MARY Q. STEELE has written many popular books for children under the pen name Wilson Gage. As Mary Steele she has written *Journey Outside* (a 1970 Newbery Honor Book), *The First of the Penguins,* and most recently, *Because of the Sand Witches There.*

Mary Q. Steele was born and raised in Tennessee. Today she lives in Signal Mountain, Tennessee, with her husband, William O. Steele, who is also a writer.